Rachel

Rachel

BETHANY HOUSE PUBLISHERS
MINNEAPOLIS, MINNESOTA 55438
A Division of Bethany Fellowship, Inc.

Bible verses are taken from *The Living Bible*, copyright 1971 by Tyndale House Publishers, Wheaton, Ill. Used by permission.

Rachel
Leila Prince Golding

Library of Congress Catalog Card Number 88–71304

ISBN 0–87123–963–9

Published by Bethany House Publishers
A Division of Bethany Fellowship, Inc.
6820 Auto Club Road, Minneapolis, Minnesota 55438

Printed in the United States of America

Dedicated to

Parents of my granddaughter, Rachel,
for whom
This book was written,
Kevin and Mary-Ellen Golding
Serving the Lord
with
Wycliffe Bible Translators

Acknowledgements

My deep appreciation to
Kathleen Carlson,
Who typed the manuscript
from my legal-pad scribbles.

And to those behind the scenes
at Bethany
Who did the fine-tuning,
My heartfelt thanks.

Springflower Books (for girls 12–15):

Adrienne
Erica
Jill
Laina
Lisa
Marty
Melissa
Michelle
Paige
Sara
Wendy

Heartsong Books (for young adults):

Andrea
Anne
Carrie
Colleen
Cynthia
Gillian
Jenny
Jocelyn
Kara
Karen
Rachel
Sherri
Stacey

Chapter One

Rachel squealed with excitement, her blue eyes sparkling as she rushed into the kitchen, her long blonde hair bouncing on her shoulders.

"Mother, look what came in today's mail!"

Mrs. Hoekstra turned from the stove, her eyebrows raised, as Rachel rushed on.

"The Marlows have invited me to be Nedra's guest for two weeks on their trip to Europe. We're to leave right after graduation next week—if it's okay with you and Dad, that is."

"I'm sure we'd have no objection, Rachel, but—"

"I know I'd planned to get a full-time job right away, but I'll never have another opportunity like this," Rachel added. "Mrs. Marlow said she'll phone you as soon as they get back from a business trip later this week."

Rachel's mother lowered the flame under the stew. "This can simmer a little longer. I made tea knowing you'd be home about now if you didn't stop at the library. How about a cup while we talk?"

"Okay," Rachel answered, wondering why her mother didn't seem to share her excitement. "Let's have it here while I make the salad for you."

"Fine, honey. Dad thought he'd be home early," Mrs. Hoekstra said as Rachel washed her hands and took salad greens out of the refrigerator.

The fragrance of mint rose around them from the steaming cups of tea. When she put the squat yellow pot down and reached for her cup, Mrs. Hoekstra had a tiny crease between her brows.

"Caroline called this afternoon."

"Caroline?" Rachel sipped the hot tea carefully to avoid burning her mouth.

"Yes, the lady you call Aunt Caroline, the one we met at Great-aunt Esther's home one Christmas when you were small."

Rachel nodded, recalling the round black face and lovely smile of the bustling lady in Aunt Esther's kitchen who had said, "Just call me Aunt, child—everyone does."

When Rachel asked her mother later about the woman, Mrs. Hoekstra had answered, "Oh, no, honey, she's not a servant; they've been friends since childhood. Aunt Caroline's mother was a cook in the home a generation ago, but these two work together to make Aunt Esther's tourist home a pleasant place for travelers."

Rachel looked up from the lettuce she was tearing into the yellow salad bowl. "What did Aunt Caroline call about?"

"Great-aunt Esther tripped on the back steps and broke a hip," Mrs. Hoekstra answered.

"Oh, Mom!" Rachel's voice was full of concern. "Is she going to be all right?"

"We hope so, but Aunt Caroline said Esther has seemed rather frail this past year with frequent chest colds. I suppose there's a chance of complications when a person is already weak."

"Is Aunt Caroline staying there with her?" Rachel asked.

"She said she would as soon as Esther is released from the hospital, but she won't be able to handle things alone. And Esther's insisting on coming home immediately, even in the shape she's in."

Mrs. Hoekstra chuckled. "She's always been a feisty lady and may get her way if they can get someone to help take care of her and Mulberry Inn."

Mrs. Hoekstra paused to sip her tea. "That's where you come in, Rachel; it's mainly why Caroline called."

"Where *I* come in?" Rachel got up from the table to slip the salad into the refrigerator.

"Yes, for some reason your Great-aunt Esther wants you to come and help out there."

"But, Mom, why me? Except for a few Christmases in her

home, I've never been around her; we hardly know each other." Rachel's voice was not only puzzled, but had a sharp edge because of the sudden pressure from this unexpected request. "Surely you don't expect me to pass up a free trip to Europe in order to care for an old lady I barely know. I haven't had any nursing experience, either; what help could I be?"

"I realize that," her mother replied quietly. "But remember, my Aunt Esther has no children, and she told me last Christmas you were the only one of her grandnieces and nephews who ever wrote to her or even sent thank-you notes for the little gifts over the years."

"She is a dear, I suppose, Mom," Rachel admitted, a bit ashamed of her outburst of selfish excuses. "I do care about her even though I don't know her well. And I *am* sorry she's injured, but to expect me to go now . . ." Rachel's voice trailed off as she stared at the tea getting cold in her cup.

Then she suddenly stood up and announced, "Excuse me, Mom, I'd like to be alone for a little while; I'm going to my room."

Mrs. Hoekstra's voice followed her daughter out of the kitchen. "I understand, Rachel, but don't be long; we'll want to eat as soon as Dad arrives, because he has an early meeting this evening."

Upstairs, Rachel sat on the edge of her bed gazing through the window between yellow ruffled curtains. Below her, in her mother's flower garden, several sparrows were pecking over the small areas of soil that had been cleared of last autumn's leaves. Early tulips—red, yellow and pink—towered over the industrious little birds, but Rachel only vaguely noticed their beauty. Her mind was nursing feelings of self-pity at the thought of exchanging a European trip for a time of nursing an old lady—no matter how kind and thoughtful she'd been to Rachel.

Hearing her father's car door slam, Rachel rose with a sigh and, after several minutes, went downstairs.

"Hi, Dad," she said, slipping into her chair at the kitchen table, after noticing her mother had already set it and was putting the finishing touches on the salad.

"What are you looking so down about?" he asked. "You've been so happy and excited lately about finishing school."

Before she had time to answer, her mother said, "There's

no reason to be upset, Rachel. After all, it's *your* decision to make."

"What's her decision?" Mr. Hoekstra was getting curious.

As though she hadn't heard him, Rachel answered her mother's comment. "But you *do* think I should go, don't you?"

"Go where?" Mr. Hoekstra broke in. "What's going on?"

"You tell him, Mom," Rachel said. "I don't feel like talking about it right now."

Her mother nodded, ladling stew into the bowls. "Well, actually, two unexpected things happened to Rachel today—one happy and exciting, the other, just the opposite."

"Yes?" her husband prompted as she paused while passing the blue-and-white bowls of steaming meat and vegetables.

Mrs. Hoekstra replaced the lid on the tureen before answering.

"Nedra Marlow's parents have invited Rachel on an expense-paid trip to Europe right after graduation."

"Why, honey, that's great," he beamed at his daughter while passing the big salad bowl to her.

Rachel said nothing, giving him a forced smile before transferring a portion of the crisp greens to her salad plate.

In the ensuing silence, he looked a bit bewildered. "Aren't you happy about that, Rachel? I'd expect you to be bubbling with excitement."

"Tell him the rest, Mom, and see what he thinks," Rachel answered, pouting a bit.

"Let's have Dad ask the blessing on the food first, so we can begin eating before the stew gets cold," Mrs. Hoekstra suggested, bowing her head.

Following his "amen," Mr. Hoekstra picked up his fork and looked inquiringly at his wife. "Now, what's happened to dampen our girl's happiness over the trip invitation? Was it cancelled?"

"No, dear," his wife answered; "I received a phone call from Caroline Wolcott—Aunt Esther's broken her hip."

"Aw, the old dear," Mr. Hoekstra sympathized. "Is she going to be all right?"

His wife laughed lightly. "Actually, she's doing amazingly well, and insists on leaving the hospital."

"Well, that's good news—what's the problem?"

His wife looked at Rachel eating silently. She wouldn't lift her eyes to meet her mother's gaze. "There's no way Caroline can handle the inn and care for Aunt Esther. Caroline's children will be in school for several weeks yet, and it's impossible for me to get away since I have my part-time job at the dress shop. You know we need that extra money to help clear up the bills from your pneumonia last winter."

Her husband nodded. "That sure set us behind, dear, but if you feel you should go—"

"No, Dad, that won't be necessary," Rachel broke in. "I'm feeling more selfish by the minute."

"Why should you feel selfish, honey?"

"Because Great-aunt Esther specifically requested that I come, Dad, and I've been very grudging about it, not wanting to give up my chance to go to Europe."

Her father nodded, chewing a forkful of salad, and her mother added, "Caroline said Esther not only hates being in the hospital, but is concerned about the costs, and probably couldn't afford to have a nurse come to her home."

"It's at times like this," Mr. Hoekstra said, "that one wishes he had extra money to share, to be able to help in a practical way."

"Well, we haven't; Aunt Esther will just have to stay put for a while, poor old dear," Mrs. Hoekstra said. "Unless—" She gave Rachel a questioning look. "I know it's asking a lot, but Aunt Esther was very good to us when you were a baby. She loaned us money for Dad to get his advanced degree; didn't charge us near the interest the bank would have, either."

"Okay, Mom," Rachel sighed. "I'll seriously consider going, though I sure don't want to right now."

"Good girl," her dad said quietly, reaching over to pat her hand.

"Thank you, Rachel," her mother added, relief in her voice. "I'm glad you'll at least consider it. I know it'll be a real sacrifice if you do give up the trip, but for some reason, I don't feel you'll regret it."

She smiled warmly at her daughter. "I've learned there's a great deal of reward, of satisfaction, from denying oneself in order to benefit someone else."

"Right you are," Mr. Hoekstra affirmed. "And I've discovered the Lord often uses the circumstances of our sacrifice to bless us in some unexpected way."

"With that kind of convincing pressure," Rachel laughed uneasily, "how will I be able to refuse?"

"Well, now, I sure didn't mean to pressure you, honey. "But, to be honest, we *are* trying to sway you toward what we feel might be right in this situation."

"I know, Dad, and I suppose you're right, but—"

"Listen, honey, just relax," he comforted her. "You think it over and pray about it tonight. Your mom and I will pray, too, asking God to guide you in your decision. After all, He knows the particulars about Aunt Esther's situation, as well as the trip. There may be some reason for you to go to Europe at this specific time, even though to us it looks like it would only be for your pleasure."

"That's true," Mrs. Hoekstra said thoughtfully. "I was so concerned about Aunt Esther, I hadn't thought things through."

"That is another way to look at it, isn't it?" Rachel brightened with new hope.

A little later, during their dessert, Mrs. Hoekstra commented, "It hardly seems that almost five months have passed since we were at her home for Christmas. We had such a nice time, it reminded me of our first Christmas after we were married." She put her hand on her husband's arm.

"It brought back a lot of happy memories from my childhood, too," he answered, then chuckled. "Lots of my cousins were usually there, and we'd spend the early evening trying to scare each other with the passed-down stories of the house being haunted. In that big old house kids could easily be convinced that some mysterious secret lurked in its depths." He chuckled again.

"Dad, you've never mentioned that before," Rachel remarked. "That must have been fun. Kids seem to enjoy scaring each other for some reason. I remember Nedra and I trying that every Halloween when we were small."

"How quickly the years pass," her mother said sentimentally. "I wonder if Aunt Esther will be with us for many more Christmases."

"No reason why she shouldn't," Mr. Hoekstra stated. "If she's getting along so well from this accident, she'll probably have lots of Christmases yet."

Later that evening in her room, checking through her closet to decide on travel clothes for Europe, Rachel thought about last Christmas.

In order to reach Great-aunt Esther's home in Indiana, they had driven northeast from earliest dawn throughout Christmas Eve day and arrived in a winter wonderland of glistening new-fallen snow.

They eventually left the congested, high-speed super highway for a two-lane blacktop that took them through numerous small and mid-size towns bright with colorful holiday decorations.

At dusk it had begun snowing heavily again, and they had to drive slowly behind a snowplow through the little community of Wedgewood, twinkling with strings of vari-colored lights swinging in the wind between blurred streetlights. Finally able to pass the plow on the outskirts, Mr. Hoekstra had driven cautiously, amid swirling flakes, along the road that curved toward the Tippecanoe and Mulberry Inn.

Although the plow had obviously been through earlier, the side road back to Aunt Esther's rambling house was fast drifting closed. As they carefully turned into the inn's drive, his wife gave a pronounced sigh of relief. Suddenly, their compact car slid sideways into a drift and stalled next to a weathered sign that read "Tourist Rooms."

In exasperation, Mr. Hoekstra hit the palm of his gloved hand against the steering wheel. "Well, that's that—looks like we have to trudge the rest of the way. You two bring the gifts, and I'll get the luggage," he said, snapping on the interior lights.

A pounding on the car's roof accompanied by a "Hello, there!" interrupted him and he quickly rolled down his window.

"Mr. Hoekstra, I'm Matthew Archer, a neighbor; looks like you've got a problem." The face of a man in his early twenties, topped with a heavy red stocking cap, smiled at them as he bent to get his head to their level.

"We've been watching for you. Aunt Caroline sent Aaron

over to get me, thinking you might get stuck out here. We've got a path shoveled to the house, but you'll have to hurry before it drifts over. I'll guide your wife. Aaron can help carry your things."

The face of a black teenage boy appeared at the window momentarily before Mr. Hoekstra opened his door and handed a large plastic gift-filled bag through the opening.

"My wife put the packages in this bag thinking it might be bad weather. She didn't want the wrappings ruined."

"I'll get 'em to the house for you," Aaron grinned, his mittened hand reaching for the bulging bag.

Rachel grabbed her overnight case and climbed out of the car, glancing at the broad-shouldered figure beside her. "Thanks for helping us," she said before following Aaron's stocky little shape through the swirling snowflakes and cold, biting wind.

The porch light welcomed them, its glow transforming the old mansion's wooden gingerbread scrolls into what looked like swirls and spangles of giant ice-and-snow cake decorations.

Not since she was a tiny girl carefully positioning cookies and milk under the tree for Santa had Rachel spent such an intriguing Christmas Day.

The large dining room table, extended its full length, had been laden with turkey and ham, corn bread and giblet gravy, vegetables, relishes, pies and bon-bons—its circumference surrounded by happy faces of black, white, and one of light olive with slanted eyes.

Because the husband of Great-aunt Esther's friend, Caroline, had recently died, she and her orphaned grandson, Aaron, and teenage daughter, Tassie, had been invited along with an elderly oriental widow they all called Grandma Ching.

Following the sumptuous dinner and gift opening, the three young adults went to a nearby sloping hillside with ten-and-a-half-year-old Aaron, returning tired and filled with laughter after hours of sliding and snowman-building.

That evening as the moon was rising, Matthew took Rachel for a delightful ride between banks of glistening snow in a small open sleigh that had been his grandfather's.

During that hour a new friendship began to grow, as Matthew confided his hopes for a short career in professional baseball before going into teaching, another career that interested him.

"I've gone through college on an athletic scholarship," he had explained, "including this last year. I've gotten a few enticing tentative offers already, but nothing's definite."

Rachel's thoughts returned to the present as she took several outfits from her closet and spread them out on the bed.

Maybe I'll check with Nedra first and see what she plans to take along, Rachel mused, her glance taking in the open letter on her dresser.

But as she reached for the phone, the remembrance of Aunt Esther's accident and her longing to be home pressed heavily on Rachel's mind. Almost afraid of what might be required of her, she knelt beside her bed.

"Lord," she prayed quietly, "you know how much I'd like to go on this trip. It doesn't really seem fair to be put in the position of having to choose between it and Aunt Esther, but I do want to do what is best in your eyes."

As she paused, words almost audible flashed into her mind, words she'd read and heard preached about many times: "I was sick and you visited me . . . Whatever you have done unto the least one you have done it unto me . . ."

After a few moments, Rachel rose, calmly took the letter from the dresser, and sat at her desk. Getting an envelope and sheet of notepaper from the center drawer, she began to write:

Dear Mrs. Marlow,
    Thank you for the invitation to join your family on your trip to Europe.
    Although my parents and I appreciate your thoughtfulness, I must decline because of . . .

Shortly afterward, Rachel sat with the stamped, addressed letter in her hand thinking about Great-aunt Esther and the people she'd met at Mulberry Inn last Christmas.

Her thoughts lingered on Matthew Archer and the letters they'd exchanged over the months since then.

It'll be great to see him again, she thought to herself, her outlook brightening.

If he's home from college and doesn't have to leave for train-

ing somewhere, she reconsidered, her eagerness dampening.

Well, I'll find out when I get there, she decided. *I'd better tell Mom and Dad I've reached a decision so they can let Aunt Caroline know I'll be coming to Aunt Esther's.*

The day following graduation ceremonies, Rachel said goodbye to Nedra before boarding an interstate bus that would take her to Indiana.

According to plans made during a phone conversation, Caroline Wolcott would have someone meet Rachel. When the bus pulled into the space in front of Tinbell's Ice Cream Shop under an overcast sky, Rachel was delighted to see Matthew Archer emerging from a ten-year-old red station wagon.

By the time she descended the steps, he was waiting at the bus door to take the small blue suitcase she was carrying. He greeted her with a happy grin—the light mist that was falling tightening the waves of his thick brown hair, causing Rachel to believe he must have had curly hair as a child.

"Hi, Matthew," she smiled, relinquishing the suitcase.

"Hi, yourself, it's great to see you again." His gray eyes crinkled at the corners, enhancing his sincere welcome. "I had just arrived from Purdue when Aunt Caroline phoned about you coming."

The drive from the little town took them past freshly plowed fields and small forests of green trees. Farmhouse yards flashed bright reds and yellows of late tulips and the bright greens of new lettuce and onions in vegetable gardens.

When the two-lane road curved close to the Tippecanoe River, Rachel could see the dark water moving swiftly between the sloping banks below.

The wide angular form of Aunt Esther's Victorian-era home was tucked away in a stand of pine and clusters of mulberry trees, its tall round turret the first detail glimpsed from a distance.

Toppled-over daffodil greenery sprawled in faded hues along the edges of the driveway. But near the house, spears of iris blades had pushed above the dark soil, among patches of late purple and white crocuses and the previous autumn's leaf litter.

Aunt Caroline threw open the front door to meet Rachel as she mounted the steps to the wide veranda that swept around three sides of the house. Her black face beamed a · lovely welcoming smile.

"I'm so glad you're here, child! That Esther is in a real dither waiting for you."

Putting an arm around Rachel's shoulders, Caroline led her into the spacious entrance hall and lowering her voice said, "The dear old thing's been home since yesterday forenoon; sure looks peaked to me, and weak as a kitten."

"If that's Rachel out there, bring her in quickly, Caroline," a frail, high voice called from a nearby room. "And bring us some tea, please."

Great-aunt Esther was resting on a chaise lounge in a downstairs bedroom, just off the front parlor. Dressed in a soft blue flannel bedjacket over her gown, the lower half of her was covered by a puffy down comforter—its patchwork colors long since faded. Beneath a fluffy bun of white hair piled on top of her head, her once dark eyes, now clouded by pain and age, brightened when Rachel entered the room. Esther Simon, a blonde-haired beauty as a young woman, held out frail, blue-veined hands in welcome, a sweet smile forming on her colorless lips.

"My dear, I'm so happy to see you. As soon as you've freshened up, do come and sit with me for tea."

After a gentle hug of greeting, Rachel went back through the front hall where Matthew was putting her luggage. "Thanks, Matthew, I appreciate your help," Rachel said with a smile. "Will I see you again soon?"

"Sure hope to," he answered with a nice grin. "I'll give you a call tomorrow around noon, okay?"

He called the next day. They agreed on a time a few days later during Aunt Esther's nap time for a drive around Wedgewood and the surrounding countryside to acquaint Rachel with the area.

That afternoon together merged with their last Christmas-formed acquaintance and their correspondence since to form a growing friendship.

After checking with Aunt Caroline to make sure she and her seventeen-year-old daughter, Tassie, would be able to spend the evening with Aunt Esther, Matthew invited Rachel to an early spring concert in the park at Wedgewood the following weekend.

Late Saturday afternoon, Rachel dressed early for her date, happily anticipating an evening with Matthew and, for her, the new experience of an outdoor concert.

Aunt Caroline and Tassie had already arrived. Aaron, Caroline's grandson by a deceased daughter, was with them.

Rachel and Tassie chatted together, renewing their acquaintance—Tassie sharing her anticipation of the following autumn when she'd be a high-school senior.

After a while, Rachel excused herself and went to Aunt Esther's room to read to her, as she'd been doing each evening. When dusk fell heavily enough that she had to turn on a lamp in order to continue reading, she knew Matthew was due to arrive any minute. A while later, glancing at her watch, she realized he was quite late.

"You look mighty pretty in that bright blue pants and sweater outfit," Aunt Esther remarked, glancing approvingly at her. "You look so much like me at your age; I must get out my photo albums sometime soon so you may see the resemblance.

"Of course, in my day, we didn't have the casualness of slacks for women and always had to contend with long petticoats and skirts. Clothes seem much more sensible nowadays."

Just as she finished speaking, they heard the phone ring, and Tassie's voice answering, then Caroline's.

In a few moments Caroline hurried into the room, then stood silently a minute, concern on her face, her hands clasped tightly together.

"Yes, Caroline?" Aunt Esther questioned.

Caroline turned to gaze worriedly at Rachel.

"I'm afraid young Matthew isn't going to keep his date with you, child. He was halfway here when his station wagon— there was a drunk driver—"

Caroline's heavy figure moved slowly to Rachel's side. Rachel felt a hand on her shoulder and heard Caroline's voice. "That poor boy is in the hospital, unconscious, he is. No tellin' yet whether he'll live."

Chapter Two

Rachel was silent, unable to speak, her mind stunned with the realization of what she'd just heard. Her thoughts came alive then, whirling in her consciousness.

Matthew dying? It couldn't be true! Not big, strong Matthew, so full of life and fun.

"Who phoned?" Aunt Esther asked.

"His daddy. He sounded all broken up, poor man. His wife told him to phone us soon's possible, knowin' Rachel was expecting him."

"They're fine people," Aunt Esther declared. "How like them to think of others when their own hearts are breaking. I've known the family many years. Matthew's granddaddy and I were schoolmates in the little one-room school that used to stand near the head of the river. It was so long ago . . ." Her frail voice trailed off.

"I think we best get her settled for the night," Caroline suggested, her work-worn dark hand patting Rachel's shoulder before she moved to the other side of Esther's bed.

Rachel nodded. "I don't suppose they'd let me see Matthew if I went to the hospital?"

"No, child, I don't imagine. Mr. Archer, he said they'd phone in the morning to let us know."

"I told him we'd all be prayin' for Matthew," Caroline added, "and for him and his missus and their great worry. The Lord's the only one who can help them now."

Tears glistened in the lamplight, running softly down Caroline's usually serene dark face as she bent to minister to Esther, her white-haired, pale-skinned friend.

Rachel felt the wetness of tears on her own cheeks and

brushed them away, wishing she could swallow around the lump that seemed to have formed in her throat. Her chest felt heavy with sorrow as, laying the Bible aside, she rose to assist Aunt Caroline.

Later, in her pajamas, Rachel knelt by her bed upstairs, pleading with God to spare Matthew's life. Time passed without her realizing, so intent was her prayer. She woke hours later chilled and stiff, and crawled into bed, pulling the comforter up under her chin in clenched fists, sobbing softly until she again fell asleep.

Rachel woke at dawn and went to stand at one of the lace-curtained windows looking out at daylight just breaking over the yard below.

Her eyes felt puffy from the weeping of the night before, and she opened the window a bit from the top, letting in a cool breeze that blew refreshingly across her face. The calls of early rising birds reached her ears, the reminder of a new day.

No matter what happens to Matthew, or what may have happened during the night, Rachel thought sadly, *life will go on for the rest of us, one day after another.*

Sighing deeply, she pulled on her robe and padded downstairs in the faint early morning light. Not knowing how to pray about Matthew, or whether he was even alive, she interceded instead for his parents, people she'd never met.

"Give them your strength, Lord," she prayed softly. "Enable them to bear whatever it is they must face today and in the coming days."

Then as she reached the big half-dark kitchen, she added, "If Matthew's still alive, I ask the same for him."

Flicking on a small light over the sink, Rachel made coffee, and while it brewed, went quietly through the house to check on Aunt Esther. Rachel found her still sleeping soundly, snoring quietly because her dentures were in a dish next to her spectacles on the bedside stand.

Rachel tucked the covers around the thin shoulders of the frail form, thinking, *She said I resemble her at my age. It's hard to realize I will one day be like this, old and weak.*

She tiptoed back to the kitchen. The chilly linoleum made

her wish that she'd put her slippers on before coming down-stairs. The chill on her feet reminded Rachel of a visit here when she was a very small child. It was before Aunt Esther had been persuaded by the family to replace her big iron kitchen range with a white-enameled electric model. Rachel thought wistfully of that stove's comforting warmth, of the faint aroma of wood smoke that emanated from it.

Wrapping herself in the blue and white afghan from the big wood rocker in the corner, Rachel curled up in the chair where she remembered being rocked during that almost for-gotten long-ago time. Tucking in her feet, she flicked on the nearby lamp and picked up a small Bible and her steaming coffee cup from where she had put them on a small table. She sipped her coffee while reading from the book of Psalms.

Except for the low rhythmic ticking of an old clock on the wall and the soft whisper of pages being turned, the kitchen, the entire house, was silent around her as she read psalm after psalm. Then she came to: "I love the Lord because he hears my prayers and answers them. Because he bends down and listens, I will pray as long as I breathe. Death stared me in the face."

Rachel stopped reading, the reality of Matthew's condition pressing against her.

She was anxious for the hours to pass, wanting to hear from Matthew's father. Yet she dreaded the call and the sad news it might bring.

Tears welled in Rachel's eyes. She knew she had to be honest with herself, to brace herself for the possibility that she might lose forever the dear friend she had so recently found.

Sighing deeply, she brushed away the tears now slipping down her cheeks and looked up to see Aaron's sturdy little pajama-clad figure in the doorway.

"You okay?" he asked, hesitating on the threshold.

Rachel nodded, setting the Bible aside next to her empty cup on the little end table.

"What are you doing up so early?" she queried.

"It's not too early," he answered. "It's kinda dark yet, but I heard a bird singing.

"Well, it may be *some* early," he grinned, rubbing his eyes.

"But I was hungry . . . and I'm scared for Matthew, afraid he's going to die. I like him a lot."

"I know how you feel, Aaron," she said, unwrapping herself from the afghan. "You cuddle up in the rocker while I make some hot chocolate and toast—how does that sound?"

"Sounds great," he said, curling up in the chair as she vacated it and went to an ancient porcelain cupboard for ingredients.

When chocolate was warming in a blue and white granite saucepan and bread waited in the toaster to be pushed down, Rachel told him, "I'm going to run upstairs for my slippers—be right back."

"Okay," Aaron acknowledged as he pulled the fluffy warmth of the afghan up around his head, his dark eyes peering happily at her. "You're nice, Rachel. I'm glad you're here. My mom likes you a lot, too."

"Thanks, Aaron." Rachel smiled at him as she turned to leave the kitchen. "I like you, too."

Several hours later, after the tall grandfather clock in the front hall had struck nine, the phone rang.

"Miss Hoekstra, this is Charles Archer. I've been with Matthew all night and wanted to call you before going home. He's still unconscious, but his vital signs are stable. My wife and I want to thank you folks there for praying for him. It gives us strength knowing others are praying with us for his recovery."

"We've been very concerned, Mr. Archer, and we'll keep on praying for him," Rachel promised, thanksgiving flooding her heart at the knowledge that Matthew was alive.

"What could I do to be of some help to you and your wife?"

"Nothing right now that I can think of, but I appreciate your offer," he answered.

"Please let me know when there is something I can do, Mr. Archer. Maybe I could sit with Matthew a while so he wouldn't be alone when you and your wife need rest. He means a lot to me."

"That's a good suggestion," Mr. Archer replied. "I'm sure my wife will be relieved knowing of your willingness—we have no relatives in the area.

"And from Matthew's comments," he continued before

hanging up, "your friendship is important to him, too."

That afternoon after Great-aunt Esther had been bathed and made comfortable and was propped in her bed with some tea, her Bible and other favorite books, Rachel felt a need to get away by herself for a while.

While the tea was being prepared, Aunt Caroline had arrived from her home a short way upriver from the inn. She declared she was going to sit with her friend Esther, and later prepare supper, so Rachel could have a short rest.

Expressing her thanks with a smile and warm hug, Rachel dressed in wool pants and a heavy hooded cardigan for a walk down to the river, something she'd not yet had time for in her busy days here.

Even though it was already spring on the calendar, the overcast day was cold. Low clouds, prodded by a chilly wind, moved across the sky.

Rachel left the house by the back door, its scroll-embellished screen door still protected against the cold with a cover of plastic sheeting.

Crossing the large backyard, she skirted an overgrown herb garden and the mound of a rock garden encircling a sunken, dry fishpond in its center.

Off to the left was a sturdy-appearing stone building, which Aunt Caroline had explained was the old carriage house when Rachel had noticed it through a kitchen window one day. Beyond it sat a large barn, its red paint well-weathered.

Rachel walked through last autumn's dry leaves, crunching them beneath her ankle-high leather boots, until she reached the rail fence that separated the yard from a wooded area. Pushing open the gate that gave entry to a path beneath the trees, she found herself strolling beneath rangy old oak trees, their bare limbs reaching outward and upward like skinny black fingers against the gray sky.

Rachel knew her concern over Matthew was coloring her thoughts and the way her eyes were perceiving things, and she mentally shook herself.

The Lord answered our prayers concerning Matthew's life, she thought. *I should be happy about that and not so depressed. But he's still unconscious; that must be a bad sign.*

Rachel's worries distracted her from noticing the tightly curled ferns that had pushed through the cool, spring soil and were standing like troops of bright green apostrophes among the dead leaves.

The path led her beneath a group of lacy little dogwood trees, glorious in their covering of white blossoms, to the beginning of a flight of stone steps. They led down the side of the steep incline to the river rushing along below.

Rachel stood at the edge of the bluff awhile watching the dark water which reflected the dullness of the day. Then she proceeded slowly down the stairway, her hand occasionally resting on the weather-smoothed log railing that ran along the left edge.

Halfway down she noticed the level area, just large enough for the stone bench that had been terraced into the side of the steep hill just at the right edge of the stairs.

Rachel brushed dry leaves from the bench and sat down. She was glad for the great silence that, except for the rushing water of the stream, filled the air around her; it suited her mood.

I would have enjoyed boating here with Matthew, she thought, *or fishing, if he liked to do that.* She chided herself then, realizing she was thinking in the past tense.

Directly overhead, the melodious call of a bird broke into her melancholy thoughts. Glancing upward, she caught sight of a robin perched among the pink blossoms on a limb of a redbud tree.

Rachel rose and stretched, a bit chagrined that a tiny creature of the wild had to remind her to consider God's blessings of this day, rather than dwelling on the worries and bleak possibilities.

Turning, she hurried back up the steep steps, noticing this time the soft plush mosses edging the stone.

I'll phone the hospital and see if I can find out Matthew's condition, she decided.

When she entered the kitchen, Aunt Caroline's ample figure was moving easily between refrigerator and sink, stove and counter. The tantalizing aroma of browning meat and onions filled the room, making Rachel's mouth water. She realized she'd eaten almost nothing all day.

"Mmmm, sure smells good, Aunt Caroline. What can I do to help?"

"Set the table, if you want to; Tassie an' Aaron and I will be eating with you and I'll stay overnight."

Deftly turning the meat with a large meat fork, she added, "Charles Archer phoned—wants you to call him at the hospital, room 207."

"Thanks, I'll do that before setting the table."

Rachel hurried from the kitchen into the wide front hall and toward a small alcove where the phone was located.

Slipping into the small upholstered chair, she noticed Aunt Caroline had thoughtfully written the hospital's number on a scratch pad by the phone.

It took a few moments to get through the hospital switchboard to Mr. Archer. Rachel was relieved to hear less tension in his voice.

"Thanks for returning my call so quickly," he said. "I've decided to take you up on your offer to sit with Matthew for a while. The doctors and nurses assure us there's no need for the family to be here, but we feel better knowing someone close to him would be here if—when—he awakens."

"He's still unconscious?" Rachel asked, her voice weak at the thought.

"Yes, he's in a deep coma; the doctors are giving us no real hope for recovery, but we keep hoping, trusting it may be God's will to return him to us.

"Our church is having a special prayer service for him this evening. That will be an encouraging atmosphere for my wife and me—its been a heavy strain. The service is scheduled for seven o'clock."

"I'll be at the hospital by five," Rachel assured him. "You'll have time then to go home for a short rest and supper before the meeting."

"Bless you, Miss Hoekstra, for your thoughtfulness," he declared before hanging up.

Rachel heard the courthouse clock striking five as she thanked Tassie for the ride into town in Aunt Caroline's old pickup.

"Phone when you're ready to come home," Tassie called as Rachel pushed the door shut. She nodded, turning to climb the wide steps.

Because of the heavy cloud cover that day, dusk had already fallen and lights were on in the hospital. Rachel stopped at the desk for a pass into the intensive-care unit, then hurried up the flight of stairs to the second floor.

The distinctive smell of a hospital made her feel a bit queasy. She wondered briefly why it always did that to her, deciding it probably stemmed from her short stay as a child for a tonsillectomy, and the remembered smell of the anesthetic.

No Admittance warned the sign of 207's door; Rachel tapped lightly. After a few moments a nurse with a small cart of supplies opened the door.

"Miss Hoekstra?" she asked quietly.

Rachel nodded, entering the room after the nurse had opened the door wider and moved into the hall with the cart.

Mr. Archer stepped forward to greet her from where he stood by his wife, who was seated next to the bed. He was a broad-shouldered man of medium height, his thinning sandy colored hair graying at the temples.

"It's nice to finally meet you." He took her hand in a warm clasp, his deep voice lowered to just above a whisper.

"I'm sorry it had to be under these circumstances," she answered as he helped her slip out of her jacket.

He nodded, then with a hand on her shoulder guided her across the room and to the other side of the bed. "Nan, this is Matt's friend, Rachel Hoekstra."

The small dark-haired woman acknowledged the introduction with a sad smile, then rose and hugged Rachel. "Thank you for being here, dear. Matthew speaks highly of you. I had been looking forward to you visiting our home soon with him . . ." Her voice trailed off, ending with a small sob.

Rachel patted Mrs. Archer's arm, thinking of nothing to say in comfort, but Mr. Archer put his arm around his wife's shoulder, leading her toward the door, her coat and purse over his other arm.

"We'll be back in a few hours to take over," he told Rachel.

"No need," she answered, following them to the door. "Why don't you just phone or stop in a moment after the service if you want to? I've decided to stay until morning so you two can get a night's rest. Please," she added, as Mrs. Archer started to protest. "I'll keep close watch on him—I'd very much like to do this for you."

Mrs. Archer nodded to her husband, and after helping his wife into her coat, he gently gripped Rachel's shoulder, tears in his eyes.

"Thank you again. I'll let you know later about staying."

When the door had closed behind them, Rachel walked slowly back to the bed where Matthew lay, pale and quiet. The only sounds in the room were those of the monitoring equipment and his breathing.

Rachel sank into the armchair that was close against the bed and peered into his face.

A faint shadow of beard darkened his strong angular jaw; his eyes were closed except for very narrow slits.

Rachel wondered if he was seeing anything, if he could hear what went on around him. She recalled reading somewhere that sometimes people in an apparent coma *are* aware of their surroundings, but are unable to say so.

"Matthew," she whispered self-consciously into the quiet room. "Matthew?"

Then taking his limp hand in hers, she stroked it softly. "Matthew, it's Rachel; can you hear me?" His fingers didn't move, but lay quietly. There was no flicker of his lashes, no indication whatsoever of any awareness on his part.

If it wasn't for his breathing, I'd think he was dead, Rachel thought miserably. *How horrible this must be for his parents.*

Later, after phoning Tassie and speaking with Mr. Archer, Rachel settled in for a long night of waiting and watching, hoping and praying.

Several times she read to him from the New Testament she'd brought along in her purse, thinking that if he *could* hear what was spoken in the room, she wanted it to be something worthwhile, something that might comfort him where he was in his silent prison. "What a wonderful God we have— He is the Father of our Lord Jesus Christ, the source of every mercy, and the one who strengthens us in our hardships and trials. And why does He do this? So that when others are troubled, needing our sympathy and encouragement, we can pass on to them the same help and comfort God has given us."

The night seemed very long, with only occasional interruptions as nurses came and went, checking the patient and equipment. Around ten o'clock someone brought her a sandwich and a cup of coffee.

But other than that, there were just the faint sounds of traffic outdoors, and a few times the distant sound of a siren. It would grow louder and louder in its eerie wailing that terminated at the emergency entrance below on the opposite side of the building.

Rachel could hear, too, the footsteps sometimes passing the slightly open door, and after daylight, doctors being paged over the intercom.

But inside the room where Matthew lay, the seemingly unending night had held only his breathing and the sounds of the mechanisms that monitored his vital functions, the assurance that he was still alive.

During the next few days, Rachel's phone calls to the hospital brought the same discouraging response, "No change." On Thursday she could hear the resignation in Mr. Archer's voice, "The doctor said Matthew seems to be weakening."

"We must continue to pray," Rachel answered into the phone, trying to prod her own weak faith. "Please, Mr. Archer, don't stop praying."

"I won't," he said, his voice flat. "I know I should say 'your will be done' to the Lord, but I can hardly bring myself to say that." His voice caught and after a moment, Rachel heard the click of his receiver.

We say it sometimes, Rachel thought. *But I wonder if we ever really mean it.* Sadly she went upstairs to her room and dropped to her knees beside her bed, oblivious to the warm breeze blowing the curtains, the happy song of a wren.

The call came the next day when Aunt Caroline was telling Rachel about Aunt Esther's small business. She had just said, "Right after her Ted and my Josiah died during the same year, she began renting a few of her rooms. She hired me to do the cooking for dinner on the days boarders were here."

The phone rang three times before Rachel could lay aside the gown she was mending for Aunt Esther and rush to the hall to answer it.

"This is the hospital. Mr. Archer has asked that you come to his son's room as soon as you can."

"Is he worse?" Rachel asked. "Is he gone?" But the person on the other end of the line had already hung up.

Her heart heavy, Rachel went to tell Aunt Caroline and ask if the area had taxi service.

"Tassie should be home from school by now," Aunt Caroline said, rising with effort from her chair. "She was to be there only a few hours today getting ready for tonight's commencement. I'll have her come by with my car and take you."

"Oh, thank you," Rachel answered, turning to go upstairs. "I'll be ready when she gets here."

Rachel climbed the front steps of the hospital slowly, not feeling the spring sunshine that warmed her bowed head. She dreaded the thought of entering Matthew's room, of hearing the words she would probably be told.

Reluctantly she went down the hall, tapped hesitantly on the door of 207, and started to push it open. Then she stopped, realizing the quiet room no longer held the eerie punctuations of monitoring machines; her heart suddenly felt as though it, too, had momentarily stopped.

Hearing Mr. Archer's "Come in," Rachel pushed the door farther and stepped inside.

Seeing the two white-coated men beside the bed across from Mrs. Archer, Rachel started to turn and retrace her steps back out the door, but Mr. Archer strode forward from where he was standing by the foot of the bed.

Startled, Rachel saw that he was smiling, his hand outstretched to her.

"Matthew wants to see you; that's why I phoned."

"See me?" Rachel was finding it difficult to take in the joyous truth that seemed evident on Mr. Archer's happy face. Not only was Matthew still alive, he must be improving!

By now Mr. Archer had taken her arm and had led her to the end of the bed. "Thank you, Lord," her heart sang. "Thank you."

Rachel stood staring at the still form covered by the sheet and buff-colored blanket. Matthew's eyes were closed, and to her he didn't look any different than before, except that there seemed to be more color in his face. His hand lay still on the covers just as before.

"Matt, Rachel is here," Mr. Archer said rather loudly.

Rachel saw Matthew's hand move; then his eyelids fluttered and his eyes opened, gazing slowly over the faces around the bed until they rested on hers.

A weak smile formed on his lips; then he said, as if with great effort, "Sorry I'm so late for our date! This is no concert in the park—but you could sit here with me awhile—if someone will loan us a radio."

He paused, then continued. "We pull in a good classical-music station here—we could pretend." His hand lifted slightly. "What do you say?"

Quickly looking up at Mr. Archer with a questioning glance, Rachel saw him nod.

"That sounds great, Matthew, but we don't need a radio. I'll sit with you while you get a little sleep."

"That sounds better yet," he answered, his smile slipping, his eyes obviously staying open only with great effort.

Mrs. Archer had risen and, patting his arm, said, "Dad and I are leaving for a while, son."

But already he was asleep. "They gave him a sedative," she told Rachel. "He'll sleep awhile. He's been awake for hours, but we haven't told him yet how long he's been here."

Bewildered by the sudden change in his condition, but her face shining with happiness, Rachel asked, "What caused the change? I was afraid he—"

"Frankly, we were told not to expect him to last through the night," Mr. Archer answered, tears in his kind eyes.

"Some sort of miracle," Rachel heard the physician next to her mutter, shaking his head. "I've never seen anything like it."

"I did once," his colleague declared. "It made me realize

there's a God who does intervene sometimes in answer to sincere, unselfish prayer."

Turning to the Archers he said, "Except for some heavy bruises and cuts on his back and giving his leg time to heal, he should be fine now after a week or so of rest. But, of course, we'll want to keep an eye on him."

Accompanying them toward the door with the other doctors, he continued, "Since X-rays show no breaks at all, he should be up and getting around on his own fairly soon."

"We'll be back in about an hour, dear," Mrs. Archer told Rachel, a happy smile on her weary face.

Rachel wondered about the comment regarding Matthew's leg. It wasn't in a cast.

The rest of that week Rachel's heart felt lighter than it had for what seemed a long time. The tension of the past week disappeared, and she went about the routine of the days with silent prayers of thanksgiving and occasionally breaking into song as she worked.

She wondered once or twice about the doctor's remark about Matthew's leg and hoped it hadn't been badly bruised, which could be quite painful.

When she found time between caring for Aunt Esther's needs and preparing meals for the two of them, she cleaned a couple of the extra rooms, putting fresh linens on the beds, plumping pillows, polishing furniture and mirrors.

"Esther sometimes rents a room or two in June when tourists begin driving through the area," Aunt Caroline had told her. " 'Course it was much better before they built the bigger highway that bypasses us, 'cause she couldn't afford any advertising along the road like the motels do.

"Why," she had continued, hands on hips, "that first summer after our husbands died, she generally had most of these rooms upstairs filled every night.

"But now," Caroline sighed, "now it's mostly families who were here in those years and come out of nostalgia on their way through the area. Or an occasional salesman who happens to end his day's work in Wedgewood and asks about a good place to stay."

"I don't imagine Aunt Esther could handle the work of

more than that in recent years, anyway," Rachel had said.

"Couldn't even have done that if my Tassie hadn't been here to help out," Caroline smiled. "She's a good worker, that girl is. The arrangement gave her a summer job without having to work crazy hours at a fast-food place and was surely a blessing to Esther. I did the meals when she rented to those that wanted supper, but with my gardening and some cleaning jobs in town, that was about all I could do."

"Cleaning?" Rachel questioned. "I thought my dad mentioned you'd been an executive secretary."

"So I was for a number of years. Mr. Shedrow was transferred when the glass factory closed, and I've never been able to find a similar position. Probably could in another area, but here—well, there's a certain feeling."

"A feeling about what?" Rachel asked. "What kind of feeling?"

"A feeling about black folks. We're tolerated, but resented if we have a better employment position than some of the white people around us."

"Aunt Caroline, surely not!" Rachel exclaimed. "Are there really attitudes like that still existing—here in a nice little town like Wedgewood?"

"I'm afraid so. I used to hear remarks, but I enjoyed my work, and Mr. Shedrow often told me how fortunate he was to have someone who did more than was expected."

"You certainly are that kind of person," Rachel told her, giving her a hug. "I'm sure you could get a position somewhere else."

"Probably could have, but our home was here, and my husband's work. He was a mechanic, a good one, farm machinery as well as cars and trucks, but he'd been raised in the city and was happy to settle here in my hometown when we married."

Now, several days following that conversation, Rachel was hanging freshly laundered curtains in one of the bedrooms, thinking about the short way the attitudes of some people had come since the time of actual slavery in America.

Her heart ached for Caroline, imagining the hurts she had experienced because of her dark skin. She wondered if Tassie and Aaron had ever been confronted with such unfeeling, unfair attitudes.

Rachel was hurrying through the cleaning of this last room so she would have time to go to the hospital that afternoon to visit Matthew.

She phoned, and found out he was now in room 109. She arranged for Tassie to drive her, and Aunt Caroline to stay with Aunt Esther.

Before leaving, Rachel went in to check on the elderly lady, who had been sleeping much of the time the past few days.

But she was awake now, seeming especially alert.

"Rachel," she began, "you will never know what a blessing it has been to have you here. I've hoped very much over the years for an opportunity to get better acquainted. I want you to know I've not been disappointed in what I've seen in you. May our God richly bless your life, my dear."

Then, as Rachel bent to kiss her forehead and readjust the pillow and covers, she added, "Give my regards to young Matthew. I trust he's as fine a man as his father and grandfather."

During the drive into Wedgewood, Rachel mentioned the recent conversation regarding bigotry.

"Have you ever had problems because of poor attitudes, Tassie?" she asked.

"Sometimes," Tassie answered quietly after a long pause, pretending all her attention was needed for driving, although theirs was the only car on the country road.

"I'm sorry, Tassie," Rachel said sincerely. "I'm really sorry."

"It's okay," Tassie answered, trying to speak lightly. "It became routine to be left out of all the fun things by the time I was a teenager. But I never got to the point of accepting it; for years I kept hoping. Maybe it'll be different for Aaron. He's still young enough now that white parents don't mind their kids playing with him."

"I can imagine the disappointment and hurt you must have felt—probably still do." Rachel hung her head, feeling ashamed of the whole human race.

Tassie's head of attractively arranged thick black braids nodded slowly. "It's uncomfortable to sense that your schoolmates' 'absorbed-at-home' bigotry is thinly masked. Their friendliness is likely just an attitude they practice because it's one they feel nice people should have."

Rachel saw the glint of an unshed tear when Tassie glanced toward her. "I've not felt that way with you, Rachel. You're the first real white friend I've ever had. It's been pretty lonely all my life, we being the only black family in the area."

Rachel put her hand on Tassie's arm as they pulled in front of the hospital and she started to get out of the car. "Thanks for telling me these things, Tassie. Friends need to share their hurts as well as the happy things in their lives." Rachel learned more about that when she reached room 109. She was happy to see the bed empty, but dismayed to find Matthew sitting in a wheelchair, staring morosely out the window, the sun's rays coming through the pane, putting highlights on the waves of his hair.

"Hi," Rachel greeted him brightly, trying not to let concern cloud her face. "Nice afternoon out there, isn't it?"

Matthew twisted in the chair, turning to look at her.

"What's nice about it?" he said flatly; it was less a question than a statement.

Taken aback, Rachel was silent a moment. Then she crossed the room to stand behind him.

"What's wrong, Matthew?" she asked quietly.

"Wrong? What could be wrong?" His voice was heavy with sarcasm. "Everything's just great!"

He was so changed, Rachel wouldn't have believed it was the same person if she hadn't actually seen him sitting there.

"I haven't the slightest idea what's bugging you, Matthew," Rachel said, a bit irritated. "Would you like me to leave?"

"Leave? Sure, why not. You can walk out anytime you like."

Rachel turned to leave and had reached the door before the underlying note of despair in his voice reached through her annoyance at his attitude.

She turned back to retrace her steps, and halfway across the room she almost whispered, "Matthew, please. What is it?"

"They didn't warn me; didn't ask my permission!" His voice was low and gruff, tight with anger.

"Warn you? About what?" Rachel asked, confused.

For an answer, he put his strong, long-fingered hands on the bright metal surrounding the chair's wheels and swung around to half face her.

"This!" he spat, pulling aside the small blanket that covered the bottom half of his body.

Rachel stared at his heavily bandaged left thigh; then her gaze lowered. She realized with horror that below his knee there was nothing.

Chapter Three

"Oh, Matthew!" she gasped, dropping to one knee. Her hands grasped his shoulders, pulling him slightly toward her.

Rachel noticed his hands, the knuckles white from his intense grip.

Then as his strength seemed to drain from him, he lowered his head. His shoulders heaved heavily as slow, harsh sobs racked his body.

Rachel lay her forehead against his hair, tears streaming down her cheeks, sharing his grief.

They were huddled like this when Mr. and Mrs. Archer arrived a few minutes later.

Although she sensed Matthew wanted her to stay, Rachel excused herself and left after a brief talk with his parents while he sat sullenly silent.

The following day Matthew phoned Rachel from his room at the hospital.

"I'm sorry about yesterday," he apologized. "Please forgive me."

"There's nothing to forgive," she replied. "Don't worry about it."

"Thanks, Rachel. Anger just seems to hit me once in a while since the surgery."

They were both silent, then he asked, "Will you come visit me here again?"

"Of course."

Rachel went the next day and several afternoons following. Matthew's moods vacillated between gloomy resignation at the loss of his leg to anxiety and despair over his future.

"But you're alive, Matthew," Rachel reminded him several

times during those days. "That's the important thing. You'll learn to adapt to the change."

"I know, I know," he would answer, his voice betraying his own self-doubt.

Rachel's mornings were filled with Aunt Esther's needs and trying to spruce up the spacious yard around the old house. Originally a riverfront mansion in the early years of Indiana's settling, it was beginning to show its age and look somewhat shabby.

Rachel decided that making the driveway and front entrance areas neat by pruning bushes and tidying flowerbeds should be her first priority. She enlisted Aaron's assistance and he proved to be a willing and seemingly tireless little worker.

It was while he was edging the flowerbed at the far corner of the big house that he saw the apparition. Rachel tried to quiet his excitement, assuring him there were no ghosts around—but he insisted.

"Sure looked like a spook to me—moved through that patch of trees out beyond the old barn."

Rachel laughed lightly. "The clouds have been forming all morning; guess one of them crossed the sun and cast a moving shadow through the trees.

"Besides, Aaron, in all the ghost stories I read when I was younger, the phantoms always appeared at night, not during the day."

"S'pose you're right," he answered, not sounding at all convinced. "But it sure reminded me of that headless horseman we read about in school this year. I was thinking about it last night and it sorta scared me."

The Legend of Sleepy Hollow," Rachel said. "I remember that one, but you know the horseman was really just someone dressed to appear that way, don't you?"

Aaron grinned sheepishly. "Yeah, but it still scares me when I think about it."

"As long as you know it's make believe, it's okay," Rachel assured him. "Now, let's hurry and try to get the summer bulbs planted before the rain starts.

"I was glad your grandma didn't have to work in town today

and could be with Aunt Esther so I could get this taken care of."

"She was glad, too," Aaron said as he carefully used a sharp spade to cut the edge of the sod where it met the cultivated soil.

"Says they were friends before I was born, though Aunt Esther was a lot older."

The wind was beginning to rise, so they hurried to get done. They were finishing just as the first scattered drops of rain fell.

Gathering up their tools and the bulb basket, they started back around the front of the house, skirting freshly prepared beds edging the wide veranda.

They ran through the slanting rain as it began to pour. Disparity in age seemed to make no difference in the companionship they shared. With contagious laughter the two friends—a tall blonde young woman and a small black boy—dropped their things on the porch and burst through the front door.

They stopped short, hearing unexpected music above the sounds of the rain, strains from the old pump organ that stood between two windows in the back parlor.

Rachel had wondered as she dusted it while cleaning if Aunt Esther ever played it before her recent injury.

As they walked down the hall in that direction, Aaron said, "Mom and Aunt Esther used to sing together a lot. Mom plays by ear—never learned to read music from a page—said she still wants to learn someday."

Caroline noticed them in the mirror set into the scrolled, curved front of the organ. She finished the hymn she was playing and turned on the organ stool to face them.

"Esther asked me to play for her," she explained. "We had been humming and quietly singing some of the old songs together. 'Fraid she barely had strength to get the words out, but seemed to enjoy it."

"As soon as I clean up a bit, I think I'll read the Bible to her before supper. If she's extra weak today, she may want to go to sleep earlier this evening," Rachel said, turning to leave the room. "Thanks from me, too, for the nice music, Aunt Caroline."

Rachel entered the bedroom shortly afterward, and found Aunt Esther already sleeping. But as she lifted the thin hand to tuck it under the blanket, she realized the frail little lady, while listening to the familiar and beloved melody, had gone to meet the One about whom the song was written.

The next two days passed methodically, filled with visits by many of the friends Great-aunt Esther had made over the years of her long life. Because Rachel was the only family member present, she greeted them all.

Rachel's parents planned to join her the morning of the funeral, and she awaited their arrival with mixed feelings.

Was it really worthwhile to miss my trip to Europe in order to come here? she mused.

Could Aunt Caroline have cared for Aunt Esther without me? Was I needed here as much as everyone thought?

The more Rachel considered these things, the more certain she became that coming here was the best choice of the two.

Aunt Esther's gratitude for even the most mundane things I did for her is something I'll never forget, she realized. *And I am glad I took time to read to her every day—but all the yard work and preparation of rooms will be of no benefit to her. It was probably wasted effort.*

Then, when her thoughts turned to Matthew, she knew she wouldn't have wanted to trade the time with him for a trip to Europe or anywhere. She was glad to be exactly where she was.

But as she descended the broad front steps of the veranda to greet her parents, whose car was just entering the drive, sorrow pulled at her heart because her time with Matthew would soon end. There was no reason now, with Aunt Esther gone, for her to stay any longer.

Overcast skies contrasted with the brightness of late yellow tulips, and a baby's gurgling contrasted with the open grave, around which family and friends had gathered.

The words of the clergyman sounded strong and clear, pronouncing the assurance of every Christian:

"Yea, though I walk through the valley of the shadow

of death, I will fear no evil, for thou art with me."

For those of us who are trusting in Jesus, every dark thing in life has an aspect of brightness somewhere, I guess, Rachel thought.

As they drove from the cemetery's exit through the opened gates of an ancient iron fence, Rachel asked her father to drop her off at the hospital. Because her parents had said they were staying only until the following day, she wanted to spend some time with Matthew before her return home.

I'm going to hate leaving here. I'll miss him, she admitted to herself as she mounted the hospital steps. *It's even harder because he's so down. I thought maybe I could eventually encourage him some.*

Matthew's face brightened when he saw her.

"This is an unexpected surprise! I knew today was Mrs. Simon's funeral, so I didn't think I'd see you."

"I just came from there—saw your folks," Rachel said.

"I've missed you the past couple of days," he added, rolling his wheelchair forward to take her hand in greeting, then turning slowly to face the chair he wanted her to sit in.

Rachel told Matthew the circumstances surrounding Great-aunt Esther's death, and, at her prompting, he told her of conversations with the doctors and his parents about his leg.

"And if all goes as well as they're expecting," he continued, "I'll be leaving for a rehabilitation center in a week or so."

"That's where I'll eventually get my peg leg," he added ruefully, turning his gaze away from her to stare unseeingly out the window.

"Pegs aren't used anymore, Matthew," Rachel chided. "You know that very usable artificial limbs are produced now."

"You're right, Rachel," Matthew conceded. "Guess I'm feeling sorry for myself again."

"Well, I'm sure I'd probably react the same way, but I read a verse in the Bible the other day that seems to fit situations like this," Rachel said.

"I don't recall exactly where it is, but it tells us it is God's will for us to always be joyful and to give thanks in all circumstances."

"I've read that before, too," Matthew commented sharply.

"But how can I be expected to be thankful for losing part of my leg?"

"It doesn't say you should be thankful *for* the sad, difficult things, Matthew," Rachel explained earnestly, leaning forward in her chair. "But that we are to be thankful *in* every circumstance. Evidently God expects us, His children, to be joyful in our relationship with Him. He wants us to be thankful for everything good, and not dwell morbidly on the hard things that happen."

"That's easy to say when you're not the victim, Rachel," he countered. "I have nothing to be thankful for—my career is ruined! What can I do in this chair or hobbling around on an artificial leg?"

"I suppose you're right—that a career as a baseball player won't work, but what about coaching or some other aspect of the game? Or you could be a therapist for not-too-seriously injured players." Rachel searched for other suggestions that might get his mind off his injury for a while.

Matthew sat silently for a minute or so, then answered, his voice softening slightly.

"Thanks for trying, Rachel, but playing was my dream."

"At least think about other ways you could use your interest and experience, Matthew, and try to let the Lord's peace fill your heart so you won't feel so down. I've been praying that you would."

A small smile touched his lips, and he leaned over to touch her arm in gratitude. Speaking softly, he said, "Yes, I will. I've been all jumbled inside wanting to lash out at everyone. But I'll try; it'll just take time, I suppose."

He asked about her plans then, wondering what she would do now that Mrs. Simon no longer needed her help.

"I honestly don't know, except I'll probably go home to Iowa. That's why I made sure to stop here today; my folks plan to leave tomorrow."

"Tomorrow!"

"I don't think there's any need for me to stay, and I've got to get a job lined up."

Matthew nodded, disappointment heavy on his face.

"But it's so soon, Rachel. Today, then, is all we have and it's about over."

"For now at least, Matthew," she answered. "But we can write like we've been doing; you can keep me up-to-date on your therapy progress." Rachel tried to make her words sound bright and happy, to lift his spirits.

When Mr. Hoekstra appeared at the doorway of the room a short while later to remind her Aunt Caroline would be waiting supper for them, she bent to give Matthew a goodbye hug and heard his whispered, "Don't forget me, Rachel. Your friendship's important to me."

"And yours to me, Matthew," she replied, kissing him lightly on the forehead.

Later, during supper around the large kitchen table, Caroline looked at Rachel and said, "A few days ago, Esther had me write a letter for her. It's in the drawer of the little desk in her bedroom. She asked that I have you read it the day of her funeral; she felt sure she would go to be with the Lord very soon."

Sudden tears stung Rachel's eyes. *How sweet of her to give me a special goodbye,* she thought.

Feeling no appetite now for the last few bites of her meal, she put down her fork and got up from the table. "If you'll excuse me, I'd like to read it now."

Her parents both nodded, her mother saying, "Of course, dear."

"I'll clear away the supper things while you're in there, Rachel. We'll wait on the pie until you're back."

Rachel smiled and hurried into the large downstairs bedroom at the front of the house. It hardly seemed like the same room the frail invalid had occupied.

The large dark-walnut tall-posted bed was neatly made up with its old hand-crafted white candlewick spread covering plumped pillows.

Shades were rolled up to their very highest point, letting in the faint, slanting rays of a setting sun. The lovely small desk stood on slender legs between the two windows.

Rachel sat in the rush-seated chair, opened the single wide, shallow drawer, and removed the envelope addressed to her that lay on some other papers. Pulling the recessed area forward, she slid the two folded sheets of paper from the envelope, snapped on the amber shaded lamp, and began to read:

Dear Rachel,

When you read this, I shall already be in my eternal home. What joy!

Because you will undoubtedly want to make immediate plans, I felt it prudent to tell you now rather than have you informed at a later date by my attorney.

Attorney! Rachel exclaimed in her thoughts. *Was Aunt Esther in some sort of difficulty? And why would that concern me?*

Her gaze dropped to the last paragraph on that page:

From the bottom of my heart, I thank you for coming to help me when I was injured. Not many young girls would be willing to discard their own plans in order to care for a crotchety old woman.

Your coming proved to me once and for all that I had been correct over the years in my estimation of the type of person you are: the woman of God you are becoming— have become.

Tears came unbidden to Rachel's eyes as she realized how close she had come to disappointing Aunt Esther. She brushed them away and continued:

It was good to know I had done the correct thing and wouldn't have to make changes so near the end.

Mystified as to what she was getting at, Rachel's gaze moved to the other sheet where the letter continued:

Some time ago, keeping a life estate in it, I transferred all my property into your name.

Rachel stopped reading, her breath catching in her throat, overwhelmed by the words before her. Could it possibly be true?

She reread the line, "Yes, that's what it says all right," she said aloud. "I can hardly believe it!"

Dudley Simpson will contact you soon to discuss any necessary details and to give you the passbook for a small savings account, which was set up for your use in taking care of the house.

I trust you will be interested in making it into a well-known, comfortable and profitable "Bed and Breakfast" establishment, as I was. You will undoubtedly have good ideas for advertising when you're ready to open.

Had I a daughter or a granddaughter, I would have wished her to be exactly like you.
With much love,

Tears again threatened to fall, and Rachel could barely make out the almost illegible signature, obviously attempted by Aunt Esther as her final work.

Rachel sat for several minutes gazing out the window at the sunset-streaked sky; her hands rested on the desk and held the sheets of paper that were in a few moments of time changing her life.

Lowering her gaze to the letter, she read it again to make sure she hadn't misread some part of it, then prayed silently, *Lord, guide me in this situation so that I will use carefully this unexpected gift that has been given to me.*

Then she went back to the kitchen and handed the letter to her father.

After everyone's exclamations of surprise and well-wishing at Rachel's unexpected inheritance, Caroline was asked to stay and discuss with Rachel and her family what this would all mean.

"What a trustworthy person you are, Caroline," Mrs. Hoekstra beamed. "To know about this and not say anything."

"Esther didn't want Rachel to know ahead of time; and I guess she just wanted to know for sure that her ideas about Rachel were as she hoped."

Then turning to Rachel she said, "She wasn't disappointed in you one bit, either—said she loved you as she would have one of her *own*."

"And I grew to love her, too, in our short time together," Rachel affirmed. "She was such a dear, easy-to-get-along-with person."

Caroline's black face glistened where tears were slipping down her cheeks as she nodded. Then a small smile lifted the corners of her lips and she said, "But she could be pretty obstinate too, insisting that things be done her way. Not because it was *her* way, but because she always thought things out ahead of time, determining the best way to accomplish whatever it was that needed doing. Then, because she knew it *was* the most effective way, she insisted on it."

"You got along well with her, didn't you?" Mrs. Hoekstra asked.

"Best friends for many years," Caroline answered.

Tassie and Aaron went upstairs to bed in two of the extra rooms, and soon after, Mrs. Hoekstra got up from the table to brew fresh coffee and serve second pieces of cherry pie.

Rachel and her parents with Aunt Caroline sat for quite some time discussing the possible future of Mulberry Inn. It was finally decided that Rachel should remain there until autumn, defining plans for the inn and deciding whether she should go to college to learn how to be a good business-woman.

Caroline agreed to keep working there for the same percentage of the inn's income that Esther had been paying her.

"I'm happy you want me, child," she admitted to Rachel. "This place has been a second home to me for a long time."

It was close to midnight when the four went to bed, and the early hours of the morning before Rachel was able to quiet the dozens of thoughts and plans that swirled in her mind. She finally fell asleep to the sound of rain against the windows and wind in the trees.

Mr. and Mrs. Hoekstra said their farewells right after lunch that day and drove away in a light rain under a cloudy sky.

"Sure hope it doesn't rain much more," Aunt Caroline said as she and Rachel went into the house after waving goodbye.

"Why?" Rachel asked. "We need rain for the crops, don't we?"

"Normally," Aunt Caroline replied as she led the way to the kitchen, "but the rivers are flooding from the heavy snow melt. Our Tippecanoe River is already dangerously high, and reports are that the Flosstown Dam may not be able to hold."

"Has the property here ever flooded?" Rachel asked, concerned.

"No, you needn't worry about that, honey. The high bluff here eliminates any chance of that, but a report from the U.S. Weather Bureau late yesterday said the storm center was strengthening over Indiana, and there is a fifty-fifty chance of heavy rains. The weatherman says the Tippecanoe is continuing to rise toward flood stage. In our area folks at the base of the hill and farther along the river are often flooded."

"Can't they do something to prevent it?" Rachel inquired.

"They do build barricades along their land near the stream's edge, but a rushing, overflowing river can wear those down in a hurry."

Aunt Caroline began stacking dishes from the table while Rachel put away leftovers.

"Man and his efforts are no match for the forces of nature sometimes," Aunt Caroline added, running hot water into the sink and squirting detergent from a bottle.

"One spring several years ago, the Tippecanoe flooded over its banks and many basements and yards were flooded. Most of the roads became impassable and much of the farmland dried out too late to plant."

"I noticed the river seemed fast and sort of high when I went part way down the bluff not too long ago," Rachel said, "but I didn't even consider the possibility of it flooding; I hope it doesn't."

Aunt Caroline nodded. "We invariably hope that, but your Great-aunt Esther and I always prepared, just in case."

"But you said the water never reached this high," Rachel said, reaching for a dish towel from the rod above the sink.

"To help our neighbors, child," Aunt Caroline explained, removing a glass from the soapy dishwater and plunging it up and down in the steaming rinse water.

A fringe of fluffy suds ringed her dark wrist; she turned the gaze of her gentle brown eyes to look into Rachel's blue ones. "We prepared well ahead of time in order to share, to assist folks whose houses *were* flooded or who had to evacuate their homes because of danger from the river."

Rachel was quiet for a few moments while she polished a glass dry. Then, "I'm glad Aunt Esther was that kind of person, and that you are, Aunt Caroline."

She reached for another glass. "Should we be preparing for the possibility even though there doesn't seem to be a problem yet?"

Aunt Caroline smiled warmly at her. "I think it would be wise. I had intended to suggest that to you. We can take care of it this afternoon."

By the time they had tidied the kitchen, the rain had increased in strength.

"There are trunks up on the third floor, in the attic," Aunt Caroline said. "Look in the one nearest the head of the stairs— there're some blankets there. You can bring them down to the back hall and stow them in the wide hinged seat that's beneath the coat hooks and mirror."

"Okay," Rachel agreed. "I'll do it right now."

Aunt Caroline's voice followed her up the wide curving staircase that led from the large front foyer to the second floor. "There's a big box covered in red-striped paper full of warm hats—Esther always spent her winter evenings knitting those. When the hats weren't needed earlier, she'd send them to the Salvation Army for gifts the next Christmas."

"She was such a caring person," Rachel marveled. "I hope I always remember to be so thoughtful."

At the far end of the upstairs hall, Rachel opened a door onto a narrow enclosed stairway. A flashlight was lying on a recessed shelf and, seeing no light switch, she picked it up, flicked it on, and started upstairs.

The sound of rain was heavier now as she neared the attic. Her steps echoing on the bare wood of the stairs gave her the sensation of being in a secluded place far from anyone else.

It was a strange feeling, stranger still when halfway up the stairwell she heard something move softly on the other side of the wall.

Rachel knew she and Aunt Caroline were alone in the house, as Tassie and Aaron had gone home to take care of some chores.

The hair prickled on the back of her neck. She paused, listening, then scolded herself, "You silly thing! You're acting like little Aaron with his spooks."

Rachel laughed lightly at herself, but before reaching the

top of the stairs, she knew she had, beyond the shadow of a doubt, heard the sound again.

On the wall above the top stair the flashlight's gleam revealed a simple shadeless light fixture. She turned it on, flooding the immediate area with glaring brightness.

Directly to her right she saw the big old-fashioned trunk; to the left, the large striped box.

Rachel blew dust from the trunk's leather handle above the lock and lifted the curved lid.

Inside were stacked serviceable wool blankets in dark colors of gray, green and navy. She gathered several into her arms and made her way back down the narrow stairway and on to the downstairs back hall next to the kitchen. She deposited them in the compartment inside the antique hall seat.

Retracing her steps, several more trips emptied the trunk. Then Rachel took several grocery bags to carry the hats in, and on her last trip to the attic that day, she emptied the striped box.

Before turning off the light, she glanced around the half-dark areas beyond the bulb's illumination where boxes, trunks and discarded furniture cluttered the large expanse all the way back to the sloping eaves.

Rachel's curiosity was aroused. *It will be fascinating to come back up here to explore when I have some free time,* she thought as she went back downstairs.

Aunt Caroline had turned on the midday news and Rachel paused, listening.

And in this area the recent downpour that flooded streets and basements has turned a normally dry drainage ditch on Clevins Road into a four-foot stream.

At least seven roads are partially impassable; we urge citizens to keep away from low-lying areas if at all possible.

Residents in Hooperville have spent the morning hastily filling sand bags to ward off further damage to their flooding community.

Dudley Simpson, Aunt Esther's attorney, phoned late that afternoon, setting up an appointment for Rachel to meet with him the following day.

After the signing of various papers the next day, she asked him some questions regarding plans for the inn. His comments brought extra questions to her mind that kept turning over in her thoughts that evening. She tried to come up with some honest answers.

Would it be wisest to sell the property and use the proceeds for some other business? On the other hand, the house has character and plenty of rooms, but will I be able to make a profit, or am I liable to lose the property because I'm so new at this?

Will I be able to offer the type of hospitality that people will tell their friends about?

Am I the kind of person who will enjoy being hostess to strangers in her home day after day, most of the year?

Is this really what I want to do with my life?

Rachel prayed earnestly, asking for guidance from Almighty God, He who knew all things, who knew her even better than she knew herself.

Of one thing she felt confident; she *could* preserve at the inn the atmosphere of a comfortable home, a place of welcoming, simple comforts and nourishing meals.

Most of all, she decided, *it will be a spot of genuine friendliness, a place where folks can truly relax.*

Rachel felt a sudden sense of joy knowing the inn was something she *could* handle with God's help.

I'll just have to move slowly, but definitely, she resolved, *studying the things I need to know and accepting help where it's needed.*

Before going to bed that night, she turned on the radio in her bedroom, but wasn't encouraged by what she heard about the weather:

The local office of the U.S. Weather Service suggests that every family in low-lying areas surrounding the Tippecanoe River take every precaution against water damage and be prepared to move out if flooding becomes imminent. Keep tuned to this station for further reports.

Also, be sure to keep children away from McHenry Creek. The creek is very high where a youngster was swept away and drowned in a culvert several years ago. Again, we stress with great urgency that you not permit children to play along McHenry Creek until all danger is past.

The next morning, feeling sure now that owning and managing Mulberry Inn could be an enjoyable way of life, Rachel phoned the hospital to tell Matthew that she would be staying.

She was told, to her disappointment, that he had left the day before. Because of unexpectedly good healing on his leg stump, he was transferred a week earlier than planned to the rehabilitation center.

Since she had no hope of talking with or seeing him again before he left, Rachel instead got out a large pad of paper and a pen, preparing to jot down her immediate plans for the inn.

But before she started, she wrote a short note to Matthew, ending with a quote from the Apostle Paul. It was a verse she felt pertained to his situation, and similar to something she'd quoted to him another day—a verse she'd copied down during her morning Bible reading:

Whatever happens, dear friend, be glad in the Lord. I never get tired of telling you this, and it is good for you to hear it again and again.

After putting the letter out for the mail carrier to pick up, Rachel flicked on the little pocket radio she'd put on the table earlier. She tuned it to a classical-music station, turning it louder than usual because of the heavy rain beating against the windows.

She hummed happily along with the music while preparing vegetables for that evening's slow-simmer stew, then filled the kitchen with the delicious aroma of browning beef as she used a long-handled fork to move the small beef chunks around in the deep iron skillet.

The pan hissed and steamed when she added cold broth, spreading a comfortable sense of homeyness over the large kitchen.

Rachel had just seated herself at the table and started her list of things to do when the music abruptly stopped. There was silence for a brief moment, then:

We interrupt this program for a flood warning for people in Wedgewood, Markstown, Hooperville and surrounding vicinities.

The dam is weakening.

Families in low-lying neighborhoods of these towns are urged to evacuate immediately. The Tippecanoe River is rising rapidly.

We repeat, if you are in the low-lying areas of Tippecanoe, leave immediately!

Warning! Residents of Wedgewood, Markstown and Hooperville, please evacuate to higher ground, away from the river, immediately!

We repeat—

Rachel waited to hear no more—she was already out of her chair, rushing for the phone in the hall.

Chapter Four

"As soon as you've moved what you need to," Rachel said quickly, "come here until the danger's over, Tassie. Is there anything I can do in the meantime to help you?"

"No, thanks—Bye!" Tassie slammed the phone down in a hurry. Rachel stood their for a moment rubbing her ringing ear.

Glad the meal she had planned for her supper was easily extendible, Rachel went to the kitchen to peel extra potatoes and carrots and put together the ingredients for a pie and a pan of biscuits.

Getting greens from the refrigerator, she washed them and tucked them into a salad bag for crisping.

I've never even been through the entire house, she mused. *The next few days will be an ideal time. I can't do much outside work with it being so wet lately, anyway.*

It was late afternoon when Rachel heard Aunt Caroline's truck come up the side drive to the back of the house. She had just finished setting the kitchen table, and went to open the door that opened onto the large screened back porch.

Rachel saw that the wind had diminished a bit, although it was still raining.

Aaron jumped down from the back of the pickup, where he'd been huddled under a tarp, and dashed for the porch, dragging a large plastic bag.

Rachel held the screen door open and took the bag from the boy; then he ran back to help his grandmother with the bag she was lifting down.

Tassie got out on the driver's side of the truck, slamming the door behind her. She sprinted awkwardly toward the house with a large tote in one hand, her purse in the other.

Soon the three had dried off, groceries and personal items were retrieved from the bags, and it was decided to eat supper early.

Conversation around the table centered on the flood danger and the unexpectedness of it happening so late in the season.

"Everyone was relieved, thinking the possibility of flooding was over for this year," Aunt Caroline said. "I feel sorry for some of the folks downstream. They'll have troubles if this rain doesn't stop soon."

"We carried almost everything upstairs," Tassie said. "Except the stove and refrigerator and Mom's piano. Sure hope water doesn't come in this year."

"Well, it hasn't reached our place since you were a small child, so we'll hope for the best. We did all we could."

"Water was almost to the road down by Hawthorne Curve," Aaron contributed enthusiastically, his voice betraying his excitement.

By the time they were ready to clear the table for dessert, the rain had definitely lessened, making everyone there feel more secure, even though there hadn't been any threat to the inn.

Aaron had asked to be excused and was occupied in the back hall with some small wood cars he was building while the two young women and Caroline lingered at the table.

"An evening like this one reminds me of the time you told about, Mama," Tassie reminisced. "The night your grandpapa almost got caught. Tell Rachel the story."

Rachel looked questioningly toward Aunt Caroline who asked Tassie, "You mean the time with the Klan after the big storm?"

Tassie nodded.

"Did your entire Wolcott clan live in this area then?" Rachel asked.

"Not our family clan," Tassie answered. "The Ku Kluxers—you know, the K.K.K."

Astonishment covered Rachel's face as she echoed, "The K.K.K., the Ku Kluxers? You mean the Ku Klux Klan was active around here? I thought they were only in the South."

"Hardly," Aunt Caroline answered with a short, bitter laugh. "Small groups of them seem to have been everywhere."

Tassie confided, "Mama's told me horrible stories that have been passed down through the family about the awful things those secretive, misguided people have done."

"There's no point dwelling on those times," Caroline said. "Except that people try to learn from the past how to live together peacefully."

"I know, Mama," Tassie said softly. "But tell her anyway about your grandpapa; it does have something to do with Rachel's property here, and might be interesting to her."

"Around 1910, I believe it was," Caroline began, "Grandpapa was a young man then. His skin was very dark, as mine is, not a lighter shade as Tassie's, so he was extremely noticeable in an area where no other black people were living.

"He had been a traveling tinker, having learned the trade from his father. But when he and Grandmama married, they wanted to settle down in one spot and chose the Wedgewood area."

"And that's when he built the house we live in now," Aaron contributed from where he was playing.

"That's right," Caroline smiled through the doorway at her grandson. "He had saved enough money for lumber to build a small house; they added to it later as they were able."

"Is that when trouble started for him?" Rachel asked. "Didn't the white residents think he belonged here?"

"Oh, everything was fine for a few years. His services were welcomed, so folks were glad to have his shop in the community.

"But then, somehow the Klan got a start in one of the nearby towns and began recruiting a few of the local people."

"What happened?"

"Not much at first . . . intimidating mail once in a while. Then there was a frightening night when a cross was burned on my grandparents' lawn.

"Some of the neighbors rallied around, encouraging them, but mostly a subtle sense of mistrust spread throughout the community.

"Worried about his wife, Grandpapa sent her on the train to Illinois to visit her parents. A few days later he received a threatening note attached to a rock thrown through his kitchen window."

"What did it say?" Rachel asked.

Aaron had returned to stand by the table. "It said Great-grandpapa better leave town if he knew what was good for him."

"Did he leave?" Rachel was trying to visualize what it must have been like to face persecution.

Aaron shook his head. Rachel looked toward Aunt Caroline.

"Where would he go that could be lasting, child? His home was here; most importantly, his work. And he had several jobs waiting, so the next morning he continued working on them.

"It rained hard that day, but late that night, he heard cars out front. He looked out the window and saw them through a rainy drizzle."

"In long white robes and hoods!" Aaron blurted.

"Yes, Grandpapa didn't wait to see more, but ran through the house to the kitchen where he grabbed his coat and a loaf of bread before hurrying out the back door.

"He headed straight back across the yard and a field to the river. Then he untied an old fishing boat he kept there and shoved it out into the current, hoping if they came that far, they'd think he had escaped in the boat."

Aaron interrupted again. "Came up this way, then, didn't he, Grandma?"

"Yes, your Great-aunt Esther was a tiny girl at that time," Aunt Caroline informed Rachel. "Several days earlier her mother had taken 'the tinker,' as Grandpapa was known, to the root cellar for some kettles she wanted him to repair."

"Is the root cellar under the house here?" Rachel wondered aloud.

"No, it's underground in the corner of the yard near the kitchen garden. Because it was fairly close and the entrance was hidden by the grape arbor, he'd decided to make it his hiding place until the Klan was gone."

"Did they find him?" Rachel asked.

"No, but they did damage the house and furniture some. Grandpapa stayed down in that cellar for almost two weeks, deciding to make them think he'd left the area for good."

"What did he do for food?" Concern registered on Rachel's face for that man of generations ago.

Aunt Caroline smiled. "Fortunately it happened in October when crops were in and the food cellars were stocked. There were baskets of pears and apples, potatoes, carrots, all kinds of root vegetables, plus cabbages, squash and pumpkins.

"Grandpapa had his pocketknife with him," Aunt Caroline continued. "When he was hungry, he'd peel a carrot or potato or eat an apple. After dark and early in the morning, he'd sneak out for well water and such needs."

"I suppose a person could get along that way," Rachel commented.

"He wasn't too uncomfortable, from what he told later," Aunt Caroline went on. "He bedded down on the straw that was protecting some of the vegetables. His concern was mainly about his untended home and for his wife, away from him and expecting their first child."

"What happened to let him know when to come out and feel free to go home?" Rachel questioned.

"Well, after a week or so, your Great-aunt Esther's mama went to the cellar to deposit some late preserves she'd made— guess it about scared the daylights out of both of them." Aunt Caroline laughed good-naturedly, imagining the scene; the others joined in.

"She realized immediately what had happened," Aunt Caroline continued the story. "Having heard gossip on a visit to town the day before, she was relieved to discover him alive and not drowned, as people believed when his empty boat had been found caught on a fallen tree snag along the shore a short way downstream.

"She invited him to come up to the house and stay with them until the trouble blew over, but Grandpapa preferred staying completely out of sight, so she gave him blankets and a pillow and took meals to him every day."

Rachel shook her head, "Sounds almost like the days of the Underground Railroad."

"Yes, and it was," Aunt Caroline agreed. "Anyway, the troublemakers left town when they'd determined my grandpapa wasn't around; the locals felt sort of ashamed for their participation, I guess, because no trouble happened after that.

"Grandpapa repaired his house and went to fetch his wife. His family and your Aunt Esther's were friends in a special, shared way during the years following, all the way down to Esther and me."

"And we'll carry on that friendship, won't we, Tassie?" Rachel commented as she put her arm around Tassie's shoulder.

The next day, because it was still raining lightly and she couldn't work outdoors, Rachel began her household inventory of listing each room's contents and approximate condition of each item.

It was one of Aunt Caroline's cleaning days in Wedgewood, so Rachel and Tassie worked together. Taking flashlights, they started in the cavernous cellar under the house. They discovered a hard-packed dirt floor beneath their feet. The abundance of thick, low-hanging dusty webs made it obvious that no one had been down there for a long time.

Tassie found an ancient broom near the bottom of the steps and used it to make a path for them through the lacing of webs that hung like the creation of some giant crochet hook from the heavy timbers above.

They discovered a large stone fireplace, its hearth blackened from many long-ago fires. Clustered nearby were a rough-hewn table, sturdy rush-bottomed chairs, and some cupboards. Walls and shelves held iron cooking utensils and heavy pottery dishes, various-sized crocks and baskets.

"It's as though we've stepped back into history!" Rachel exclaimed.

"Or into a museum," Tassie added.

"Do you think these used to be servants' rooms down here?" Rachel asked.

"More likely slave quarters," Tassie remarked with a slightly sarcastic laugh.

"I suppose they could have been," Rachel said slowly. "Please don't be bitter, Tassie."

"I know I shouldn't," Tassie said. "Besides, none of that, then or now, is your fault.

"Oh, Rachel, look!" she exclaimed, quickly changing the subject because of the item her flashlight beam had just discovered. "Look at the darling baby cradle."

It was in the corner beyond the fireplace, a small resting place for a tiny child. The cradle's sides curved up at one end forming a hood that was carved with leaves and a heart, the carvings filled now with dust.

Rachel put out her hand and swept away the tangle of webs draped down from the hood. She picked up the tiny coverlet carefully, shaking off the dust to reveal the still-bright colors of the little patchwork pieces, so skillfully put together with minute stitches.

She checked a small pile of books on the fireplace mantel and found them brittle and disintegrating from age.

Sweeping the beam of her light beyond the immediate area, Rachel could make out several bedsteads. Going to investigate, she found mattresses of straw and heavy ticking resting on interwoven rope bases. The mattresses and folded quilts were heavy with dust and had been chewed by mice in several places.

Except for a number of large and small wood barrels in another web-festooned area, the girls found nothing else; they soon went upstairs to wash their hands and remove bits of web from their hair and clothes. Their minds were full of ideas about the area beneath the house.

While they enjoyed a cup of coffee, Rachel wrote down each item she'd noticed in the large cellar, from the iron skillet on the hearth to the small straw-filled mattress in the cradle.

"This big house is probably filled with the stuff of the last hundred and fifty years or so," Rachel mused aloud.

"From the casual glance I had around the other day, the attic is crammed with all sorts of things, Tassie. Looked as though there were lots of boxes and trunks. I can hardly wait to check through them."

"It'll probably be more fun than work," Tassie smiled. "Hope I can help you when you do."

"No reason why not," Rachel concurred. "Unless you'll be

busy for your mom or have a job in town by the time I get around to it."

"I won't be too busy at either," Tassie assured her. "Mama and I discussed it last night and decided I should help you get situated here, since I've already applied for jobs at all the promising places nearby."

"Oh, that's good, Tassie. I enjoy having you with me, and there may be more to do here than I planned on. I'll appreciate your help."

By the time they had inventoried the kitchen and large walk-in pantry, and what had once been the butler's area, it was time for a late lunch.

The rain had stopped; Aaron arrived to eat with them. "I've finished all the chores at home that Mama asked me to do," he told Tassie. "And boy! The water's sure getting deep in the ditches along the roads. I walked 'stead of riding my bike. I was afraid the tires would slip and dump me where the road was flooding some."

"I'm glad you were careful." Tassie spoke in her "big sister" tone of voice. "We don't want Mama worried about you."

After lunch, he slipped out of his shoes to go outdoors and enjoy the wet grass while picking up twigs and branches from the large yard.

Rachel decided to inventory the upstairs bedrooms before continuing with rooms on the main floor.

"After all," she said to Tassie as they climbed the curving stairway, "we may be fortunate and have lots of people wanting to rent rooms this summer, if I can think of an inexpensive way to advertise."

When they reached the landing, she added, "The only rooms I've been in up here are mine and the two I freshened while Aunt Esther was still here in case there were guests early in the season."

"I've cleaned them all at one time or another," Tassie said. "A few of them have extra nice furniture."

And so Rachel discovered when she opened the doors to the remaining five rooms. One held a bed with curved head and footboards; a large cedar-lined chest at the end held fringed wool blankets and hand-embroidered sheets and pillowcases. This room also had a slender curved-legged, triple-mirrored dressing table topped with ivory and celluloid dresser sets, and a chest with door-enclosed drawers.

The room directly across the hall had similar furnishings, all in fine condition. While they were writing down the contents, Rachel glanced out the window to the lawn below.

"Whose dog is Aaron playing with?" she asked.

"That's Kiepuras' Holly," Tassie answered after coming to look down at her brother tussling with the tan-and-white terrier.

"Kiepuras?"

"A retired couple from Hammond. They have a cottage a short way down the river—come here during the summer mostly. Holly runs away from their fenced-in yard every chance she gets. Aaron is delighted when she scouts around the neighborhood and finds him. They've become good friends."

"You can tell that just from watching them," Rachel observed, turning from the window to open a chest drawer.

"Holly's a gentle little dog, but she's very protective and can bark viciously when she wants to let anybody know they're trespassing," Tassie told Rachel as they continued lifting and counting the linens. Both girls admired the fine drawn-work and embroidery.

Leaving that room, they turned a short jog in the hall that formed an alcove where another door was located.

"That's not a bedroom," Tassie said as Rachel stepped inside the alcove to open it.

"It's the door to the stairs that lead to the turret room. I doubt that we'll find anything, but I've never been up there."

"Sounds interesting, but don't think we'll take time for it today."

Doors to the remaining bedrooms in the far section of the L-shaped hall were locked, as the others had been; but a tagged key she'd found in Aunt Esther's desk unlocked them.

When they opened the doors each time, Rachel gasped and exclaimed, "Oh, Tassie, look!" Then they discovered another richly decorated suite.

These rooms were much larger than the others, with oriental rugs, thick satin hangings, and a magnificent brass bed.

Towering globe-topped corner posts, gleaming in the afternoon light, caught the girls' reflections with funhouse-mirror-type distortions as they moved around the room.

Rachel fingered the crystal pendants hanging from the ruby glass shade of one of the fine oil lamps gracing the dresser.

"Just look at these delicate crocheted doilies, Tassie," she said. "And there are more in this drawer," she added, opening a top one.

The bed held a voluminous double-bed tick and pillows all plump with down and topped with a coverlet of intricately made satin and velvet patchwork edged with fine braids and tassels.

Other drawers revealed finely embroidered linens, tiny little boxes filled with all manner of things they didn't take time that day to list, and neat piles of hand-crafted, lace-edged lingerie of nineteenth-century vintage.

"I feel almost as though we've stepped back in time and are intruding on someone's privacy," Rachel commented, relocking the door of the last room behind them.

"The things in these rooms are so lovely and unusual," Tassie agreed. "You're very fortunate to have inherited this place."

"Yes, I realize that more and more," Rachel agreed.

"I hope I can figure out how to manage it the best possible way. I don't mean just financially, Tassie, but to somehow share it with others who could also enjoy the lovely things here. And the cellar would be fascinating to people. It's evidently connected with a more distant history than any of the rooms we just checked."

"Maybe you could make a sort of museum with the rooms that are especially interesting, Rachel," Tassie suggested.

"That's a good idea. Some of the things stored in the attic might be useful in that way, too."

Then she gave a light laugh. "I don't think boredom will be a problem here with all the interesting things to investigate and plans to make."

"Feeling overwhelmed might be more like it," Tassie laughed.

The late afternoon brought cloudy skies again and a letter

from Matthew. Rachel sat on the top step of the front veranda and eagerly read it.

Dear Rachel,

The things you spoke to me about are true. I'm learning I *can* give thanks to God even in this situation. Since being here, even for this short time, I've seen people in much worse situations than mine. I *am* thankful; I thank Him that some more serious accident didn't happen to me. And I'm thankful for life itself—that I didn't die in the crash; I could have so easily.

I'm sorry for my bitter attitude—I've asked God to forgive me and I hope you will, too.

I know there will undoubtedly be many adjustments and frustrations. Please bear with me and continue to be my best friend.

Love,

Matthew

Rachel's deep concern over Matthew was eased now by his hopeful, upbeat attitude. She prayed he would hold on to it during the rough days and months ahead.

A light drizzle had begun to fall when Rachel went back inside, and when Caroline returned at dusk, the rain was increasing.

"The talk in Wedgewood is that the little dam near here seems to be weakening from the pressure of the extra water," she reported. "Folks over near Hooperville have already been evacuated and those at Markstown were moved out an hour ago because the water's coming over the banks so fast now.

"I thought I'd run Esther's supply of emergency blankets over there right after supper—I doubt many of them thought to grab bedding when they left their homes. One usually thinks it'll only be a few hours before they can return." Caroline sat down heavily in a kitchen chair, easing her shoes off.

"You look extra tired, Mama," Tassie said. "Let me drive over—I'll be careful."

"I'll go with her," Rachel chimed in. "Let's put the blankets in heavy plastic bags to keep them dry and go now before it gets too dark."

With blankets piled between them on the seat and more

under plastic and a canvas tarp in the truck bed, Tassie backed the vehicle down the long drive and onto the gravel road through steady rain.

"That's strange," Rachel muttered.

"What is?" Tassie asked.

"A light in a window of the old barn."

"Not you, too," Tassie chuckled. "Aaron's always thinking he sees lights there, but far's I know, Aunt Esther's had that old building just sitting there locked and deserted for years."

"I probably saw a reflection of some sort," Rachel agreed.

Water was beginning to seep over the gravel of the road a short way downstream near one of the cottages. Through the dimness Rachel saw a lighted doorway and a door being held open for two dogs that were entering the home. Aaron often played with the smaller one.

That must be where Kiepuras live, Rachel thought.

In Wedgewood the two young women loaded the blankets into a Salvation Army van that was preparing to take food and supplies to a central evacuation point. People were being housed for the night in an old Army Reserve Center building located between the towns.

Then they headed back cautiously through the continuing rain that slanted against the windshield.

When they reached the gravel road that ran along the top of the bluff paralleling the river, Rachel opened the truck window a bit for a minute, listening.

"Sounds like the river's running high and fast." She shivered at the thought and rolled up the window.

"Even though Mulberry Inn's safe, I hate to think of what could happen to some of the cottages along here."

She had hardly finished speaking when the truck swerved sharply and she saw that Tassie was fighting to hold the wheel. Then she was in control again and they moved ahead through the rain.

"What happened?" Rachel gasped.

"I don't know," Tassie answered. "Something must have happened to the road there. Felt as though the edge had dropped away."

"Whew, that may have been a close call. We should be home now in a few minutes."

"Yes, I think that outdoor light there is Kiepuras'." But Tassie's comment ended in a shriek as the steering wheel seemed wrenched from her hand. Rachel's side of the truck tipped downward as the vehicle made a sharp half-turn and began falling and skidding down the steep bluff.

Praying silently that they'd miss any trees, Rachel suddenly thought of the rushing waters below and heard her own scream join Tassie's.

The sharp impact of a wheel against a log threw the truck end-over-end. Rachel heard a thudding splash, felt the painful jarring of her body, and sensed the vehicle, upside down, sinking in the turbulent waters.

Chapter Five

In the darkness Rachel groped frantically, realizing that the cab was fast filling with water and she and Tassie were buckled inside, hanging upside down.

"Help me, Father," was her frantic prayer. "Show me what to do!"

Feeling the strain on her lungs as she steeled herself to hold her breath, Rachel fumbled with the seat-belt clasp, finally clicked it open, and felt herself freed.

The gratitude of her heart rushed to her God.

At the same time she had already discovered, with her probing foot, that the impact had thrown the passenger door ajar. The truck had landed in the stream in such a way that the rushing water was pressing against the door, holding it wide open.

"Thank you, Lord—thank you."

During the few seconds while all this was happening, Rachel groped for Tassie and, finding her motionless, released her seat belt and somehow dragged her free of floating seat cushions blocking their way.

Her mind screaming for God's help, her lungs on the verge of bursting, she shoved Tassie out the door, keeping a grip on the girl's wrist.

They popped to the surface; Rachel sucked in a deep gulp of air, trying not to lose her grip on Tassie in the raging water.

I barely know how to swim! How will I save us? Which direction is the shore? Help us, Lord!

Rachel's mind was whirling, frantic thoughts and prayers tumbling around like the swirling waters.

At that moment, something bumped hard against her. She

realized a seat cushion had followed them out of the truck door and to the surface.

Pulling Tassie against her, encircling her under her arms with her own free arm, Rachel grasped the cushion, hoping it would stay afloat.

Fighting to keep their heads above the churning water, Rachel's gaze searched through the rain and early darkness for some identifying landmark.

A light! Must be the Kiepuras'. I've got to try to reach the shore—it can't be very far.

Soon she gasped with joy as she felt the firmness of the stream bed beneath her feet.

Rachel let go of the cushion, allowing the current to take it, and dragging Tassie, struggled through the shallower water to the shore, where she collapsed, gasping for breath.

Worn from the struggle with the angry stream, her body aching from the truck's collision with the stump and the river, Rachel reached over and shook Tassie. "Tassie! Tassie! Are you all right?"

With a groan Tassie opened her eyes and gasped, "What happened?"

Tears of pain and relief mingled with the rain on Rachel's cheeks. "Oh, Tassie, the truck—"

Suddenly she was interrupted by voices shouting and footsteps approaching.

"In the river, George! Looks like car lights shining up from the water! Hurry! Holly! Come back here! Ginger!"

Struggling to get up, Rachel heard crashing noises through nearby bushes, the whining of a dog followed by a large furry ear over her forehead, and a big tongue licking her cheek.

A man with a flashlight appeared, and in its light she saw the big dog beside her and a small terrier nosing Tassie's head, rousing her.

"Is there anyone else out there?" the man asked, helping them both to their feet.

"No, just us," Rachel answered weakly. "Tassie was knocked out, but I think she's all right."

"Come on then," he said, steadying Tassie and guiding

them through the rain to stairs leading to a wood deck near a cottage.

The two dogs had rushed ahead and were at the lighted doorway clamoring to be let in. The screen door opened and they disappeared indoors. Rachel saw someone standing just inside the door waiting to let them in.

"I'm George Kiepura," the man introduced himself. "This is my wife, Dorothy."

They stepped into the kitchen area and Rachel said to the attractive, middle-aged, dark-eyed lady, "I'm afraid we're dripping and muddy—we'll make a mess on your floor."

"That's all right," Dorothy reassured her. "It'll easily clean. Here, take these towels and dry yourself off a bit. I've started coffee."

"Holly and Ginger, get back!" George commanded the two dogs, who were shaking themselves to rid their coats of water, spraying droplets over everyone.

Pouring steaming cups of coffee, Dorothy invited Rachel and Tassie to sit at the table where they talked for half an hour, regathering their strength, before George drove them cautiously up the road along the river to Mulberry Inn.

Aunt Caroline spotted their headlights as soon as they rounded the bend near the inn. She'd been perched by the front window all evening, anxiously waiting for them to return home.

Realizing there had been trouble when the girls got out of a strange car, she threw open the door and hurried out in the rain and mud to bring them in.

By now, the girls were too exhausted to give her the complete story, so Aunt Caroline lovingly hustled them into hot baths and soothing beds.

Mr. Kiepura waited to be sure the girls were all right and to tell Aunt Caroline his version of their mishap.

"Well, thank the Lord, they're home safe and sound in their beds," Aunt Caroline sighed with relief. "I hate to think what might have happened tonight!"

"Yes," Mr. Kiepura agreed, "and to think they were just trying to help out their neighbors when they could have been safe in their own homes. People around these parts are surely going to appreciate those girls."

"I imagine they were wanting to follow the good example that Esther set for so many years. . . . Well, thank you for all your help, Mr. Kiepura, and do come again—under more normal circumstances."

The next morning both girls slept later than usual. Waking to the brightness of sunshine at their windows, they realized happily that the rain was over.

The front-hall clock was striking ten by the time they had breakfast. As the girls ate, they related what had happened the night before.

"My, was I relieved to see you girls last night! I'm so thankful you weren't hurt."

"I wouldn't have made it without Rachel," Tassie said, looking gratefully at her friend.

"I was really scared. I thank God we got out and someone saw us," Rachel returned.

After they finished their breakfast, Rachel consulted a small notebook she'd pulled from her shirt pocket.

"What do you two have on the agenda for today?" Caroline asked, scrubbing potatoes and carrots at the sink.

"I'd like to tackle the attic today," Rachel stated. "Is that okay with you, Tassie?"

"Sure—I think it'll be fun if the rest of the house is an example of what you'll find up there."

"I'm looking forward to our 'treasure hunt,' " Rachel laughed lightly. "I'm sure there'll be lots of interesting items up there. Let's get started."

As expected, they found the vast attic crowded with boxes of dishes and books; the aroma of mothballs or cedar wafted from trunks of extra bedding and patchwork. Rachel visualized a large set of wicker furniture painted white, fitted with colorful cushions, and gracing the front veranda with welcoming comfort for summertime.

They opened containers, checked contents, recorded and repacked items. By the time Caroline called them for a late lunch, they sighed with relief.

When they had finished eating, Aaron pleaded, "Can't I please go up there with you? I promise not to get in your way."

"It's crowded up there, with all kinds of boxes and things," Tassie replied. "I'm sure you'll be bored."

"Let him come, Tassie," Rachel urged. "It may be fun for him to poke around some of the things."

"All right, Aaron, come on. Actually, it's fun for me, too, even though it's tiring after a while."

Racing ahead of them up the enclosed stairway, Aaron reached the attic and immediately maneuvered his way between boxes and furniture to one of the round porthole windows.

He rubbed years of grime from the pane and shouted, "The oak trees are so full of leaves, you can barely see the old barn, even from up here!"

Then, his interest caught by a small three-drawer chest to one side of the window as the girls emerged from the stairway, he asked, "Okay if I look in this, Rachel?"

"Sure, Aaron, just handle things carefully," she answered.

After brushing dust from the surface, making himself sneeze, he opened a drawer and pulled out a couple of pillowcases stuffed with ancient clothing, which he immediately began trying on. He strutted around in a velvet vest and ruffled man's shirt, then discovered in the deep bottom drawer a top hat, which he also modeled.

Laughing at the ridiculous outfit—the shirt and vest just skimming the knees of his short legs—Rachel and Tassie set about inventorying the contents of a tall two-door wardrobe.

Aaron finally tired of the things in the chest and packed them back, placing them as close to the way he'd found them as he could.

He moved on to check the contents of a bushel basket, finding only old textbooks that had been left uncovered to the dust of decades. Finding nothing promising to read, he continued back under the eaves, poking in boxes as he went.

Then he discovered a small trunk wedged back in the farthest corner where the roof overhead sloped down to meet the attic floor.

Opening it, he saw what looked like more pillowcases, or possibly sheets. Hoping to find more dress-up-for-fun clothes, he dragged them out.

When he had his latest outfit on, he yelled across to where Rachel and Tassie were working, "Hey, look at me!"

They both gasped in astonishment and horror.

Before them stood, in white robe and pointed hood covering his face, a dwarfed version of a member of the Ku Klux Klan.

Chapter Six

"Who-o-o, e-e-e," Aaron vocalized ominously. "Who-o, I'm a ghost."

Loathing written across her face, Tassie rushed toward him, shouting, "Aaron, get out of that thing!" She grabbed him by the shoulders and shook him soundly. "How could you, Aaron! Don't you know what that is?"

Tears welled up in the young boy's eyes as his aunt jerked the hood off his head.

"What'd I do?" he asked, his voice trembling, tears beginning to glisten on his round black cheeks. "I didn't mean no wrong, Tassie; what's the matter?"

"It's all right, Aaron," she answered, calming herself and pulling him to her, patting his shoulder. "I'm sorry—you couldn't know."

"Couldn't know what? What's going on, anyhow?" he cried, pulling away from her, surprised to see tears in her eyes, too.

"I'll let Mama tell you. Let's get you out of this robe."

The enthusiasm of all three deadened by the experience, Tassie took the disgusting outfit and shoved it back into its hiding place, and they trooped dejectedly downstairs.

Delicious aromas drifted toward them as they neared the kitchen and Aaron sniffed in loud appreciation.

"Boy, smells like baked ham—potatoes, too—and hot biscuits."

He rushed down the hall into the kitchen, gave his grandmother a quick hug around the waist, his hands a cursory wash at the sink, and plopped into his usual chair at the table.

"What's wrong with you two?" Caroline asked as she turned from the oven and saw the girls' faces.

Rachel gave Tassie a questioning glance and, seeing her quick nod, said, "We'll tell you while we eat, if that's all right, Aunt Caroline. We'll be back soon as we freshen up."

On their way down the hall to the bathroom next to Caroline's room, Rachel whispered, "I hate to tell her what we found, Tassie, after the account of her grandfather's experience with the Klan."

Tassie shocked Rachel with her response. "And she didn't tell you the really bad part, Rachel. The Klan killed her great-uncle, her grandpapa's brother. They hung him for nothing more than saying good morning and tipping his hat to a white lady as they passed on the sidewalk."

Rachel listened with growing horror as Tassie's voice lowered, slowed, and she seemed reluctant to go on.

"They came just after dark—with their torches—did it right in front of his screaming wife and crying children—left him swinging in their front yard. The neighbors were afraid to help his wife cut him down till morning; she was a tiny little lady and couldn't do it herself."

By now, Tassie had slumped down on the edge of the bathtub, hands gripped together. Her shoulders shook as her voice droned on.

"Oh, Tassie!" Rachel exclaimed, sitting beside Tassie and putting her arm around her shoulders, her heart and voice filled with compassion for the other girl's hurt for her family of generations ago.

Later, sitting at the supper table discussing man's inhumanity to other men after the story had been verified by slow, sad nods of Caroline's head, Rachel asked, "Why didn't you tell me this story instead of the less terrible one about your grandfather, Aunt Caroline?"

"I didn't ask her to, because it's too awful to think about most times," Tassie interjected.

"She's right, Rachel," Caroline affirmed. "It's something difficult to consider without hatred. I don't want my family to have hard feelings toward, or be uncomfortable and fearful with, other white folks who had nothing to do with those past times."

Rachel glanced slowly around the table at the familiar

black faces, seeing only love in their eyes for her. With all her heart she wished there were a way to erase the frightening, sad happenings from their minds.

Aloud she said, "Finding the Klan robe was a real shock to me, too, Aunt Caroline. Do you have any idea whose it was?"

"Sure don't, honey, but Esther may have. I vaguely recall her making some comments years ago that didn't make sense to me then. Now, in the light of your finding the outfit, they do."

"What comments, Mama?" Tassie asked.

"I don't exactly remember," her mother told her. "But I got the impression that she felt some sort of guilt by association when past Klan activity in this area was mentioned by someone. We never actually discussed it, so I'll never know."

Caroline sighed. "Let's forget that subject now and hope it's forever in the past."

Turning to Rachel, she said, "Mr. Archer phoned while you girls were in the attic. He'd like you to return his call when it's convenient."

"Thanks, Aunt Caroline—I'll do it right now." Excusing herself, Rachel hurried to the phone in the hall.

"Mr. Archer, this is Rachel Hoekstra."

"Mrs. Archer and I are planning to drive over and visit Matt at the rehabilitation hospital this Sunday; wondered if you'd care to go with us?"

"Oh, yes, I would, Mr. Archer. When should I be ready?"

"Plan to leave about seven a.m. We'll attend services at the chapel there. We'll stop by for you."

Returning to the kitchen, Rachel shared her news, then said, "Aunt Caroline, I've had your truck on my mind all day. Were you able to make arrangements for having it pulled from the river?"

"Joe down at Arnow's Garage said he'd try to get at it tomorrow. There've been so many problems for folks around here, he can't make time until then. Don't you worry about it, though. I'm just thankful you girls are all right."

By the following afternoon a crowd of several dozen people had gathered to watch the retrieval of the old blue pickup from the swiftly moving river.

Aaron had been warned by his mother not to play near the stream until the level was again normal, but he begged permission for Rachel and Tassie to take him to see the spectacle. He watched with excitement as the wrecker with *Arnow's Garage* emblazoned on its doors jockeyed into position at the edge of the road on the bluff above the river.

"Sure hope they don't have problems getting it out," Tassie said as she and Rachel watched the two men in swimming trunks making their way gingerly down the steep slope.

Dragging heavy ropes behind them, they waded into the swift current, then swam to the submerged vehicle and disappeared beneath the water's surface.

"They'll fasten those big hooks on the truck's frame," Aaron contributed, nodding his head importantly.

Tassie grinned at him. "I suppose you wish you were down there helping them."

"Yeah, that would be great!"

The two men were swimming back now, and once in shallow water signaled to their assistant in the truck. The motor started, roared, then the gears of the drum began to mesh, and slowly, very slowly, the ropes were wound, pulling the truck over into an upright position. After the men positioned the hooks, the vehicle was towed toward the shore.

Its faded blue paint shone with wetness in the sunshine as it broke the surface and was pulled through the shallow water.

The adults in the crowd clapped; the children, jumping up and down, cheered. Slowly but steadily the dripping truck was dragged up the bank, over the top of the bluff, and onto the gravel road.

With Aaron running ahead, the girls walked over to look at it.

"The keys are still in the ignition!" he exclaimed, peering into the window.

As the girls passed the wrecker, its motor finally droning to a stop, one of the men called, "Tassie, your mama asked that we take the truck into the garage and check it over. Tell her everything seems intact so far, except for a dented roof."

"Okay," Tassie answered. "Thanks."

Back at the inn, Rachel discovered that a couple from Iowa had arrived, interested in a room for one night.

"They're patrons from a year before last," Caroline informed her. "I told them we're not doing dinners yet, and maybe won't, but suggested one of the restaurants in Wedgewood. They'll be back later. They wondered if perhaps they could have a simple breakfast here tomorrow morning."

"I'm sure we could arrange that without much trouble," Rachel answered, a little excited at the thought of her first paying guests. She hurried upstairs to double-check one of the rooms she had prepared while Aunt Esther was still alive.

She opened the window to let in the breeze that softly moved the curtains and draperies. Then she hurried outside to gather a bouquet of flowers for the dressing table.

The guests were a pleasant middle-aged couple who chatted amiably throughout breakfast about their family and interesting travels. Rachel was glad to have something new to talk to Matthew about when she saw him on Sunday, hoping to get his mind off his problems.

But her concern was unnecessary, because on arriving at the Rehabilitation Center that day, they found Matthew smiling and happy, eager to take them on a tour of his temporary home.

He took them first to the room he shared with several other young men, making Rachel feel more like she was being shown around a college campus of active youth than a ward of disabled people.

"I'm so happy for you, Matthew," she declared as they went out into the hall, heading for one of the therapy rooms. "You're not depressed at all, and you seem so enthusiastic about everything here."

"You're right, Rachel," he agreed, deftly rolling his chair along beside her.

"I know you'll be relieved, too, Mother and Dad," he added, turning to them as they walked along on the other side of his chair. "I'm deeply sorry for the worry I've caused you, for the hurtful things I said."

"We knew it was just a shocked reaction from finding your leg gone, son," Mr. Archer answered, putting his hand on Matthew's shoulder. "We understood." Mr. Archer paused a moment, then said, "The Bible speaks in the Psalms of situations like that—I believe it's the tenth verse of Psalm 14. It says: 'Only the person involved can know his own bitterness or joy—no one else can really share it.' "

Mrs. Archer dabbed at her eyes with a handkerchief, a shaky smile on her lips.

"Yes, we could certainly understand the backlash, but you did worry me for quite some time, Matthew. I'm so glad God got us through that phase of your recovery."

"To be honest, Mom, I'm glad it's in the past, too. I got plenty disgusted with myself when I'd think back on things I'd said and I'd make up my mind that it wouldn't happen again. But then the awful reality would hit me again and the discouragement would flood over me—next thing I knew I'd be griping, complaining, and getting terribly angry."

Matthew stopped his chair, looking lovingly into the face of each of them. "Thank you for hanging in there with me. Just having you by me with your quiet understanding, just knowing that you were praying for me, gave me strength to decide to keep on trying."

Rolling his chair forward, he went on, "I want to show you some of the machines I've been working out on. The next door on the left has a good selection for strengthening and rebuilding whatever each of us needs to work on."

"Why, except for missing limbs, these young men look just like fellows working out in a gym anywhere in the country," Mr. Archer remarked, voicing his amazement as he followed Matthew and the ladies into the large room and stood just inside the door.

"They are just like guys anywhere, Dad," Matthew assured him. "They just have to work harder, find ways to make up for what's no longer there and learn to use replacements in order to do things that others can do without even thinking about it."

"Right he is!" remarked a nearby red-haired teen lifting a weight with his prosthetic arms. "You agree, don't you, Moe?"

he asked, pausing and glancing at the boy at his side.

Moe nodded. "I try to always remember on my bad days something I read that Abraham Lincoln once said. It was his observation that people are just about as happy as they make up their minds to be. Pretty good thought, don't you think?"

Rachel smiled at him, happy that Matthew had friends with such positive attitudes.

The next two days Rachel reserved for finishing the attic inventory.

Monday evening, Aunt Caroline mentioned to Rachel the "Food-Crafts-Antiques Fair" to be held in the park at Wedgewood on the Fourth of July.

"I always take candied violets and rose-petal jam," she said. "I prepared the violets early this spring, and I'll work on the jam tomorrow morning."

"I'd like to watch you do the rose-petal jam. I've never heard of it before," Rachel said, smiling.

"Maybe you'd like to help me," Aunt Caroline suggested. "It's an enjoyable task. I'm especially glad to do it because the proceeds from the sale of it and the violets go to stock the *Help the Needy Pantry* at our church."

"What a nice idea!" Rachel exclaimed. "Does the church have a booth at the fair or does someone sell for them?"

"We have our own booth," she answered. "A large one. We try to carry a variety of each thing the fair promotes—food, crafts, antiques."

"Ummm," Rachel mused while acknowledging Aunt Caroline's explanation.

After a few moments, she asked, "Do you suppose they would like to sell some of the things from the attic?"

"What kinds of things, honey?"

"Oh, there are lots of old books; I could categorize them if any seem to have interesting titles. And there are vintage clothes for both men and women. Maybe children, too—I've more chests and boxes to check," Rachel answered.

"My!" Aunt Caroline declared. "We've not had an assortment like that for many years. We usually have just a few crystal or china pieces that have been cherished as family heirlooms."

"Good!" Rachel said decisively. "I'll work in the attic to-morrow and see what else I can find."

"Bless you, Rachel." Aunt Caroline gave her a hug. "You gather together what you feel you'd like to contribute; then Tassie and Aaron can help carry them down here."

"Most of the wool and cotton things will probably smell dreadfully of moth balls," Rachel warned, doubt creeping into her voice. "Will that offend folks and keep them from wanting to buy?"

"Oh, that should be no problem at all; we'll just hang those things on the clothesline outside, and they'll air out in no time."

"Good!" Rachel answered.

"What's good?" Aaron asked, coming into the kitchen where the two were talking. "Something in here that needs tasting?"

"No," his grandmother laughed good-naturedly. "But there are some extra cookies in the jar if you're hungry."

"What's so funny?" Tassie came in the back door carefully carrying a quart container brimming with rose petals, which she put in the center of the table.

"Just your nephew's appetite," Caroline answered. "My, those are nice," she added, leaning her housedress-enveloped roundness over the table to peer through her bifocals at the sweet-smelling petals.

"Don't they have a marvelous perfume," Rachel sighed, taking slow, deep breaths above the rose petals.

"There are more, too, Mama," Tassie informed her. "The early bushes in the garden back by the carriage house are doing really well this year. But I know this is the amount you need for a batch of jam. I'll gather more when you're ready."

"I'm glad you just brought this many for now. They'll keep better on the stems until I can get at them. Fortunately, the weather forecast predicts clear and mild for the next week or so."

As soon as they'd had breakfast the next morning, Rachel and Tassie headed up to the attic, taking several large, clean cardboard boxes with them.

Rachel went right to the heavy walnut chest of drawers she

was going to check when Aaron had made his upsetting discovery a few days earlier.

"Wonder what these are?" she questioned as she opened the shallow top drawer and lifted out several cloth-wrapped bundles.

Sitting on an old round piano stool that had glass balls beneath the metal claw feet of its legs, she began to unwrap one.

"Look, Tassie, postcards," she said, beginning to sort through them.

"Here's one commemorating the 1893 World's Columbian Exposition in Chicago, and it was sent by someone named Agatha," she added, holding it out to Tassie.

Unrolling the cloth from around another package, she said, "These seem even more interesting; lots of holiday greetings. Aren't they lovely?"

Tassie sat on a crate beside her, and the two went quickly through the piles of cards they were uncovering from their wrappings.

"I've heard there are folks who make a hobby of collecting old postcards," Tassie commented.

"Me, too," Rachel answered. "These ought to be of interest to them—so many different kinds. Look at this pile; it seems to be mainly of Indians and of blacks, and these are of politicians."

"I like these best, don't you?" Tassie held up a group picturing chubby, frilly-dressed Victorian children and fluffy baby animals playing among flowers and butterflies.

"Yes, and these, too," Rachel answered. "Look how pretty these are." She had just unwrapped the last packet, which revealed valentines. They were decorated with cherubs and birds, sewed and glued-on lace and ribbons, lovely with ruffles, swags and bows, all containing sweet verses and sentiments.

"Let's take these downstairs and look through them more thoroughly tonight," Rachel suggested, beginning to put them into one of the boxes. "Your mother will enjoy them, I'm sure. She may know whether anyone has offered things like this at the fair."

"I haven't seen any there," Tassie said. "In fact, I've never seen any before; they're a nice discovery."

"I'll finish the drawers in this chest, Tassie," Rachel decided. "You might want to do that trunk over there. I brought an extra pad and pen so we can check and record separately."

"Good idea," Tassie said, reaching for the pad and pen. "We can do a quicker inventory that way." She laughed. "I could probably spend all morning just on those postcards. These things from past generations are so fascinating."

"I'm glad you're enjoying this, Tassie, 'cause I am too," Rachel answered, smiling at her friend.

As Tassie turned away to move to the trunk along the opposite wall, Rachel tugged open the next partly stuck drawer and lifted out several carefully wrapped velvet-covered photo albums. The richly padded red covers, now slightly faded, had brass corners and snaps—one with a tiny lock and a key attached by a silk ribbon.

Sitting cross-legged on the floor, she opened the cover of one, intrigued by faded sepia photographs and tintypes. Rachel quickly became engrossed, forgetting the job at hand. She was startled back to the present by Tassie's chuckle and, "Oh, Rachel, look at these."

Looking up from the last album, Rachel recognized the articles of clothing immediately.

Rachel grinned. "Look here; I was just glancing through pictures of people dressed in that same kind of beachwear, wondering what it must have been like to swim with those outfits on."

"Let's try them on," Tassie suggested impulsively with an impish grin.

Rachel hesitated only a moment before saying, "Okay, let's." Putting the albums in the box with the postcards, she got up from the floor and went to where Tassie was bent over the opened trunk. A blue-and-white striped article of cotton-knit clothing was draped over its edge.

"I'll use that one," Tassie said as Rachel picked it up to inspect it. "It looks pretty small and I'm skinnier than you are."

Tassie held up a smaller hand-knit version. "This might fit Aaron—call him, will you?"

"Okay," Rachel answered. "The way he loves trying things on, he should really enjoy this," she added, heading for the stairway door.

Because the girls were wearing lightweight shorts and sleeveless tops in the early July heat, they felt they could pull the out-of-date fashions on over their clothes.

They were struggling into the hot knit clothes when Aaron clattered up the stairs and burst into the attic.

"Found some more costume kind of stuff, huh?" he grinned. "Some for me?"

With only one leg in the tight blue-and-white striped knee-length trunks, Tassie stopped long enough to hand him the two pieces of what appeared to be a child's outfit.

Aaron held them bundled against his chest. Then, feeling suddenly modest in front of the girls, he stepped over behind a tall wardrobe.

Rachel and Tassie couldn't resist snickering as they observed each other's progress in dressing.

"Look's like all you'd be able to do in that getup is float— or sink," Tassie teased, giving Rachel a once-over. "Though I must admit that white braid trim does look pretty against the navy blue on your high collar and those ruffly puffed sleeves."

Rachel giggled. "It's this full skirt over the knee—covering pantaloons—and these slippers with attached lace-to-the-knee leggings that blow me away. I don't wear much more than this in a snowstorm."

Then, giving Tassie a smirking glance, she added, "You look as though you *are* wearing someone's winter outfit— skier's longjohns."

Aaron sauntered from behind the wardrobe just then and gave them an exaggerated pose in his wool suit of short-sleeved shirt and knee-length trunks, tied at the neck and waist with ribbons.

Then his gaze took them in. His long-lashed, dark eyes opened wide and his mouth dropped open.

"These things are for *swimming*?" he asked, a low giggle escaping his lips.

Then, they all met each other's eyes and burst into gales of laughter.

When they'd caught their breath, they decided to go downstairs and model the vintage clothes for Aunt Caroline.

Rachel and Tassie were each gathering up a photo album to take along when Aaron said, "Know what I found on the bluff out by the barn today? I think its a bag of stuff that turned into a rock."

"You found what?" Rachel was puzzled.

"It was like a rock with paper glued on it," Aaron explained. "I'll show you when we get downstairs."

Chapter Seven

While Caroline heartily joined in the laughter at the old-fashioned swimsuits they wore, Aaron said, "I gotta get out of these things—they scratch something awful."

"He's right," Rachel chimed in. "And they're hot, too. I'm sure glad styles today are more comfortable."

"Actually, this one's not too bad," Tassie admitted, as the other two pulled off their woolen outfits. "I think mine's made of cotton."

"Lucky you," Rachel laughed lightly, "and the gal who wore it eons ago. I wonder why swim fashions for the women were so bulky. This one covered almost everything from my toes to my chin, except for my forearms."

"Well," said her Aunt Caroline, arching her eyebrows and shaking her head, "better that than the ultra-scanty things girls wear today."

"Seems there should be a happy medium somewhere," Tassie muttered, pulling off, with some effort, her blue-and-white knit swimsuit.

"Whew, what a relief!" Rachel exclaimed, removing the pantaloons, the last article of her outfit, and smoothing her own shorts. "Glad I don't have to put those on to swim this summer. By the way, is the river safe for swimming?"

"The current's usually too swift even when the water's at normal level," Tassie answered. "But it's lots of fun to tube-raft down to Hooperville."

"What's that?" Rachel questioned.

"Each person sits on, sort of in, a large inner tube. The current carries you along without any need to paddle. We can take a trip someday if you'd like to try it."

"How do you get back here?" Rachel asked.

"Mama drives down with the truck and meets us at the landing spot."

"Sounds great! Let's plan on it as soon as we can find a free day." Rachel's eyes sparkled as she continued. "Sounds like a cool way to spend a hot day."

Aaron came in from the porch lugging what looked like a misshapen five-pound sack of flour in a faded, discolored bag.

"See—hard as a rock," he announced, shoving it onto the table.

"Can't make out the printing except the word Paris," Tassie said. Turning the object over, she remarked, "Looks like hardened plaster of Paris here at the corner where the sack must have opened. What do you think, Rachel?"

Rachel rubbed the area with her thumb, then got a paring knife and scraped at the white surface.

"Sure seems to be. We made models from plaster in art class last year," Rachel answered. "Wonder who would have left this on the bluff on our property?"

"Flooded river must've dropped it there," Aaron surmised.

His grandmother chuckled. "Honey, the river didn't reach anywhere near up there. This piece of land is much higher even than our yard."

"Yeah, guess you're right, Grandmama," Aaron conceded, a bit chagrined as he picked up his prize to return it to the porch. "Okay if I try to carve something out of it?" he asked, looking at Rachel.

"Sure," she replied; "finders, keepers."

"Thanks," he grinned. "Could I borrow that knife, maybe? My pocket knife's at home."

"Don't know why not." Rachel handed it to him. "There are several here in the drawer, so we won't need it."

That afternoon, the girls brought down from the attic boxes of things Rachel had decided she wanted to offer at the fair— if Aunt Caroline felt they were suitable.

"There are things in one corner of the attic we haven't looked through yet," she said, putting a box of lovely hand-worked linens and needlepoint pillow tops on a chair in the dining room. "There's still a tall chest with drawers and doors, plus several boxes. I took a quick peek. It looks like mostly children's things, so I think I'll leave them for another time. Will you help me decide which of these we should put in the fair booth?"

The hours passed quickly as the items chosen were aired on a line outside. Though they still carried some odor of moth balls, they were carefully pressed and laid between sheets of new tissue paper. Seeing her mother checking her watch, Tassie offered, "Mama, I'll start the spaghetti for tonight's supper if you'd like to be getting out the things for your rose-petal jam."

"Thanks, honey," Caroline said, laying aside a dresser scarf she'd been mending, and pushing herself up from the chair. "Want to help me, Rachel?"

Rachel glanced up from the box where she was layering fancy pillowcases in folds of tissue paper. "Sure, be with you as soon as I finish this stack."

Aunt Caroline disappeared into the kitchen. Just then Rachel heard the phone's shrill ring from the front hall, and hurried to answer it.

"Matthew!" she cried, thrilled to hear his voice.

"Hi," he greeted her cheerfully. "Any chance you're not already booked up for the Fourth of July?"

Rachel laughed lightly, glad he sounded so happy. "I don't have a date if that's what you mean."

"That's it, exactly," Matthew chuckled. "How about meeting me at the fair in the park that morning?" Then, before she could answer he added, "Unless you'd like me to call for you in my wheelchair—might be a bit crowded." His voice was teasing.

"Unless you have a license for that vehicle, I think I'd just as soon meet you," Rachel answered, going along with his playful mood. "I'm going to drop some things off at the Community Church booth about seven."

"Okay, we'll eat our meals at the food booth—breakfast included, if you like. They usually have great stuff. See you then," he said, adding before hanging up, "Tell Aunt Caroline and her family 'hi' for me."

As she turned from the phone, Rachel's face was wreathed

in smiles; her heart felt happy and light as a fluff of down.

"Matthew's coming home for the Fourth," she announced, passing through the kitchen. "Said to tell you 'hi'."

"That's great! Good for him," Tassie exclaimed. "Mama's in the old butler's pantry." She waved her hand in the direction of the swinging door.

Rachel found Aunt Caroline selecting tiny jars from an assortment of various sizes on one of the shelves.

"These look like baby-food jars," she observed, taking the tray of jars Aunt Caroline handed her.

"The young mothers at the church save them for me. Esther always stored them and contributed the rose petals and other ingredients. I'd make the jam and we'd decorate the jars and little baskets together."

"Those strawberry baskets?" Rachel asked, nodding to where they were piled on a long shelf below the jars.

"Yes." Aunt Caroline gathered some up before leading the way back to the kitchen. "Four little jars fit nicely in each basket."

Later, the kitchen radio was tuned on for the evening newscast while supper dishes were cleared away. "Esther never did approve of television," Caroline chuckled. "Insisted radio was good enough for her, and cheaper, too."

Tassie and Rachel wove colorful ribbons through the strawberry baskets and lined each with a bed of Easter basket grass while Caroline gently rinsed the flower petals. Then she sat at the table, carefully removing the white petal ends.

Rachel stopped working on her basket to watch the petals being firmly packed into a pint measuring cup.

"We save this heavy old cookpot for just this jam, and a few other specialties," Caroline told her, dumping the petals into the pot. Taking it to the stove, she added a pint of boiling water and turned on the flame.

"We let this simmer about ten minutes," she said, turning to Rachel, who had joined her by the counter.

Taking several items from the cupboard, she continued. "Next we'll stir in a couple drops of this red food coloring and then strain the batch."

"Is it finished then?" Rachel asked, thinking it seemed very simple.

"Oh, no," Aunt Caroline laughed. "After the straining, we'll add about two and three-fourths cups of sugar and several tablespoons of honey to the liquid."

"That sounds more like it," Rachel laughed at herself. "Is it cooked more?"

"Thirty minutes more. Then you can stir the petals back in and carefully fill the jars."

"It's already smelling delicious," Rachel said, "like roses just after a light rain."

When the rows of little jars were filled and sealed with hot paraffin wax, Rachel and Tassie tied narrow ribbons around the necks, and then they were ready to be nestled into the baskets.

"I feel as though we've captured bits of Esther's rose garden in sparkling globes to share with others," Caroline proclaimed.

"Whoever buys these will also be sharing the most wonderful jam I've ever tasted," Rachel said, the tip of her tongue removing the last drop of pink sweetness from a spoon.

The faint lovely fragrance of roses echoed the persistent tingle she felt in her heart lately whenever she thought of Matthew.

Shortly after six the morning of the Fourth, Tassie and Rachel were carefully packing trays of beribboned jelly baskets in the back of the truck, surrounding them with boxes of linens.

"Keep an eye on them, so they don't tip," Tassie told Aaron as he scrambled up into the spot reserved for him.

Even at that early hour, cars were lined along the drive nearest the booths and folks moved back and forth between the two areas, carrying boxes and baskets as they set up their displays.

After carrying her boxes to the Community Church booth, Rachel took time to renew her acquaintance with Mrs. Ching, who was involved with breakfast preparations at the Methodist booth across the midway.

Aunt Caroline joined them, and the two older women chatted briefly about the fair. Then Mrs. Ching mentioned the current local news item.

"I understand they found the hijacked truck abandoned on that dead-end lane next to Mulberry Inn property—hidden by the old overgrown orchard, they say. Have the police questioned you?" she asked, turning to Rachel.

Rachel shook her head. "I hadn't even heard about it."

"Me either," Aunt Caroline said, "not till this morning, that is. Heard it mentioned on the news while I was fixing coffee."

"Sure seems strange, anyone wanting to steal stuffed animals prepared for the museum." Mrs. Ching clucked her tongue. "Paintings or jewelry I could understand," she said before turning back to the pancake batter she was mixing.

Rachel had just finished arranging Aunt Caroline's tiny hand-crocheted baskets of candied violets next to the larger ones of rose-petal jam when Matthew moved smoothly across the grass toward her in his wheelchair.

Her heart gave a small flip-flop when she saw him, and her breath caught as she took his extended hand, returning his happy grin. Rachel felt the quick warm blush that tinged her cheeks. She withdrew her hand from his clasp as their eyes met and she felt her cheeks grow warmer. Nervously, she turned back to the counter, pretending to be extremely absorbed in rearranging items.

"Those look too pretty to eat," Matthew commented, craning his neck to see better.

"I haven't tasted the violets, but the jam is great," Rachel said, her heart still feeling fluttery.

"I know that from past years." Matthew smacked his lips with exaggeration. "And you'll discover before the day is over, there are lots of goodies here."

"That's what Aaron's been telling me," Rachel laughed. "I'm finished here if you're wanting to get breakfast. Tassie said the pancake booth opens at seven-thirty."

The two young people spent a happy day together visiting booths, sampling foods, browsing the art exhibit set up near the bandstand, and doing lots of talking.

It was the communication that Rachel sensed was binding them together—sharing their trials and dreams. She learned of the disciplined effort he was going through adjusting to the loss of his leg, the deep frustrations and occasional small victories.

"The chaplain at the Rehab Center has been a real help to me," Matthew said, maneuvering his chair along the path beside her as she strolled through the garden area of the park admiring butterflies and drifts of flowers.

"We've become good friends—he helped me see the destructiveness of my poor attitude. Told me everyone usually has a time in life when problems seem to gang up on them that they don't feel they can handle."

"But, Chaplain Bob reminded me of something I already knew but wasn't practicing; that is, not try to do it all myself."

"Was he talking about putting it in God's hands, trusting Him to help you do what you need to?" Rachel asked.

"Right!" Matthew exclaimed. "And I'm learning to be more calm about the lack of one leg. Bob had me memorize a Bible verse he gives all the fellows there.

"It's from Jeremiah 29:11: 'I know the plans I have for you,' declares the Lord. 'Plans to prosper you and not to harm you; plans to give you a hope and a future.' "

"Sounds encouraging," Rachel smiled.

Her smile quickly faded, though, as a sense of foreboding swept over her. Not far behind them stood two men she had noticed watching her and Matthew several times that day.

Don't be silly, she chided herself. *After all, Matthew's the only person here in a wheelchair; it's natural for people to notice him.*

But that thought didn't calm her anxiety, because she remembered seeing them hanging around early that morning before Matthew had arrived.

Rachel was even more disturbed when, munching on crusty brown ribs at the barbecue stand that evening, the same men sat near them—apparently eavesdropping.

The taller, sandy-haired man stared at her in a most disturbing way. She couldn't help but notice his eyes. They were the color of cloudy pale-green water.

Chapter Eight

Rachel tried not to look at them, for although they appeared to be just a pair of nicely dressed, mannerly fair-goers, their obvious interest made her uncomfortable.

She was relieved when Tassie and Aaron joined them, sitting where they partly shielded her from the men's view.

Aaron, excited about the fireworks display that would be starting at dusk on the baseball field, soon urged them in that direction, insisting on pushing Matthew in his wheelchair.

"Okay, okay, I give in," Matthew laughed, realizing the sense of importance it gave Aaron to be able to help this older friend, someone he admired.

When he'd helped Aaron maneuver the chair to a spot at the end of the bleachers and Aaron had settled next to him, the girls just behind them, Matthew spoke. "Aaron, you told me early this spring you wanted to be just like me someday— what about now?"

The boy cocked his head, studying Matthew's face, seriously considering the question.

"Well," he finally began, "you're still you, Matt. I wouldn't want to not be able to walk, but you'll find a way around that and do what you want."

Matthew chuckled. "You have more confidence in me than I have in myself. But thanks, buddy; you're okay."

In the dim light of dusk, Rachel faintly saw the happy, contented grin on Aaron's face before his glance moved from Matthew. Suddenly he pointed toward a light on a nearby pole.

"Look at that giant bug flying around!"

"That's a bat, Aaron," Matthew informed him matter-of-factly.

Rachel had a sudden feeling of revulsion as she joined the others in trying to see what he was exclaiming about.

She observed in fascination the tiny creature moving in slow, smooth undulating flight, silently soaring and swooping around the lighted area.

"It's hunting its supper of moths and other nighttime insects," Matthew explained quietly. "Watch what happens when it spots a tasty morsel."

With the gracefulness of the raised arms of a ballet performer trailing wide, swirling chiffon scarves and coming forward to enfold her partner, the little bat's webbed wings swooped down and forward, capturing its prey with no pause in movement.

"Hey, that's a neat trick!" Aaron exclaimed.

"I always thought bats were frightful looking things," Rachel admitted; "that was a lovely performance."

"Guess if those awkward-looking animals can move gracefully, there's hope for me," Matthew commented hopefully.

"You'll do fine, Matthew," Rachel encouraged, laying her hand on his shoulder.

As the first skyrockets whooshed into the air to explode into myriads of colorful sparkles, he turned to her and said, "I hated to mention it earlier, but I'm only here for today—gotta leave in the morning. But I'd like to talk to you about your carriage house after the fireworks are over."

"All right," Rachel answered, disappointed that he would be leaving so soon, yet curious about his interest in the carriage house.

Enjoyable as the bright display was, she gladly watched the finale of glittering American flags, anxious to be alone with Matthew.

Moving slowly through the crowd, leaving the bleacher area, Matthew said to Tassie, "Will you please tell your mom that I'll bring Rachel home? That is, if you don't mind," he said, taking Rachel's hand as they paused at the midway entrance. "Dad and Mom are here, so you don't need to worry about me trying to drive."

"I'd like that, thanks," Rachel responded as she returned the light squeeze of his hand. "Give me time to see if Aunt

Caroline needs my help with anything first."

"Don't worry about that," Tassie interrupted. "I'll take care of it, but I doubt there's anything to do except throw the empty boxes in the truck. Last time I was by there, it looked like all your things were sold."

Matthew's parents were waiting at the car when they arrived.

"How nice to see you again, Rachel," Mrs. Archer greeted her, giving her a quick, warm hug while Matthew's dad helped him into the car.

"Sure is," Mr. Archer agreed heartily, turning to smile again at her as he folded the wheelchair and shoved it into the car trunk.

"Do you mind stopping for coffee and a chat?" Mrs. Archer asked as they drove out of the park's drive.

"Sounds nice," Rachel said from the back seat next to Matthew.

When they were settled around a table at Tinbell's Ice Cream Shop, Matthew turned to Rachel. "We have a proposition for you."

"Yes?" Rachel looked inquiringly at them.

"Mrs. Archer and I are selling our farm and moving to Pennsylvania," Mr. Archer explained. "I'm going to join my brother in his hardware business."

"Since I've lost my leg, I obviously won't be playing professional ball," Matthew broke in. "And I don't care to make a move from this area, at least not right now."

Rachel sat quietly, wondering where she fit into these plans. She couldn't think of any way they could use her help.

"Last year your Great-aunt Esther had me install a small kitchenette and bathroom in what is now *your* carriage house; plumbing's always been my sideline. She had in mind to have it made into extra guest space in the event she might sometime not have enough rooms available at the inn."

"And, I'm going to need a place to live when the folks leave," Matthew added. "Any chance you'd care to have it remodeled into an apartment and let me rent it until I decide what I'm going to do about a job?"

The unexpected suggestion took Rachel by surprise. The

three watched her expectantly as she sat silently pondering what to say.

Then, smiling slowly at them, she said, "It might just work out all right. I haven't even been *in* the carriage house yet. But you have, Mr. Archer—what would need to be done to get it ready?"

"Wouldn't really have to do anything except run some electricity out there. Could put up a few partitions if you've a mind to, but I'm sure Matt wouldn't mind using it as an open area."

"Partitioning it into rooms would probably be nicer," Rachel said thoughtfully. "How soon would it have to be ready?"

"Mrs. Archer and I would like to move by September first, and Matt expects to be away until around that time, so he won't need it before then."

That gives me almost two months, Rachel thought. *I wonder if I can get a carpenter to finish in that time, and if I can even afford it.*

Mr. Archer's voice broke into her reflections. "I could do the work for you; I'm kind of a handyman—I've remodeled our home. All it would cost you is the materials."

"I couldn't let you do it for no pay, Mr. Archer," Rachel insisted.

"In that case," he answered with a chuckle, "we'll consider it as something I'm doing for my son. Agreed?"

"Well, I guess so," Rachel responded hesitantly. "We can discuss that part of it later. When would you like to start?"

"I have some things to finish at the farm so it'll be ready for the new occupants; shouldn't take long. How about if I come by later this week and discuss the floor plan with you, estimate what I need, and get the materials ordered. Then, I could begin week after next."

"That sounds fine to me, Mr. Archer," Rachel smiled. "Thank you for offering to help."

"Glad to do it, Rachel. We want to know Matt's settled before we leave."

The following morning, Rachel decided to check out the carriage house.

Aunt Caroline's family had returned to their home the previous evening after the fair, so she was alone for her breakfast and Bible-reading time.

As she started down the path from the back door, Rachel noticed a pair of delicate white and yellow moths reveling in the nectar of the still-open primrose blossoms.

Rachel herself was reveling in the loveliness of the warm, clear morning and the rich penetrating fragrance of the flowers.

The weathered brick path began just beyond the mound of the root cellar at the far corner of the backyard.

Almost obscured by the overrunning bright green leaves and violet flowers of vinca-minor, the path skirted the orchard, leading through a city-block-sized pasture.

Rachel strolled through this meadow, enjoying the morning sunshine and the scattering of wildflowers—late blossomings of bluebells and pink cowslips.

"Praise Him for the growing fields, for they display His greatness," Rachel murmured, remembering part of a verse from the Psalms that she had memorized in Sunday school years before.

At the outer edge of the meadow, the path led through a small stand of maple trees where masses of purple and white violets still bloomed under the green canopy of heavily leaved branches.

Stooping to pick a small nosegay of them, Rachel tucked it into the buttonhole at the throat of her shirt.

"Let the trees of the forest rustle with praise," she quoted aloud, completing the verse.

Rachel emerged from the tiny forest that edged the stone building and slipped her hand into her jeans pocket for the key, labeled carriage house, she'd found in Aunt Esther's desk.

To Rachel's surprise, the large and rusty old-fashioned skeleton key slipped easily into the keyhole, turning smoothly.

Rachel pushed the thick wood door open and stepped into the slate-roofed stone building.

With the modern little kitchen area and small bathroom she noticed at one end of the room, she felt it could become a snug, comfortable cottage.

After walking around, envisioning room partitions and fur-

niture placement, she left, satisfied that Mr. Archer's sugges
tion had been a sound one. She was eager for his visit to get
specifications, already anticipating the finishing of the project.
She could hardly wait to furnish and decorate the little cabin.

He told her on Saturday that the roof and structure itself
were sound. A small wall furnace and wiring for electricity
would be quickly installed with the assistance of his friend, a
local electrician.

Because he expected to finish everything by August 15,
Rachel spent any free time during the next few weeks planning
the decor and ordering needed items. Mr. Archer had said
Matthew would bring his own desk and bedroom furnishings.
Mrs. Archer phoned to tell Rachel she wanted to help by fur-
nishing the kitchen with her present appliances, and whatever
else was needed for that area of the cottage.

"With what you're offering, plus things from the attic, it
looks like I'm not going to have to buy much of anything to
make it a real home," Rachel bubbled with a light, happy
laugh. Then, after thanking Mrs. Archer for her thoughtful gen-
erosity, they made a date to get together and arrange everything before Matthew's expected arrival around the last week
of August.

Rachel received a short letter from him the tenth of that
month. He wrote of his enthusiasm for the cottage and shared
his ideas about a possible job opportunity. The letter ended
with a secret. "I've a surprise for you, Rachel—can hardly wait
to tell you. See you August 25, if all goes as planned. If you
can keep that evening open, how about a light supper in
Wedgewood at Tinbell's?"

Rachel answered his letter immediately, accepting the
date, sharing his eagerness.

Before that time arrived, she and Aunt Caroline were kept
busy with guests at the inn every night.

"I'm thankful for the income," she wrote to Matthew, "and
I also find I'm really enjoying this type of work. Your idea of
advertising the inn by placing flyers at service stations on main
highways leading through this area is paying off. You and
Aaron did me a great favor in offering to distribute them.

"Tassie is training for a promised position in Practical

Nursing, and after finishing his chores, Aaron spends his time roaming through the woods and along the river, usually with the Kiepuras' little terrier. She sneaked out of the yard so often to play with him, they finally decided to just let Aaron stop by for her every day.

"Aaron said to be sure to tell you he's taught her a neat trick—carrying notes back to the Kiepuras' grandson, Michael, when he's there visiting.

"The river has dropped to what Aunt Caroline says is the usual depth for this time of year. I waded in knee-high water near the rock pier or jetty that someone built at the bottom of the bluff where our stairs end. What fun! I felt like a ten-year-old."

The day after writing that to Matthew, Rachel was busily preparing a second-floor guest room when, glancing out the window, she saw Holly darting out from the trees lining the bluff. Behind her came Aaron, running as fast as he could with what looked like a large fish under his arm.

Sure hope he's not planning to bring that big, smelly thing into the house, she thought, trying not to get impatient with him. At the same time, rushing downstairs and hoping to stop him at the back steps, she had to laugh at her own fastidiousness.

If it's edible, I should be glad to get it. Aunt Caroline will surely know how to filet and prepare it, and it'll provide meat for a number of meals, she realized, remembering her large freezer.

Rachel hurried through the kitchen, mindful of a quizzical glance from Aunt Caroline, who was preparing vegetables at the sink.

"I'll explain in a minute," Rachel assured her, laughing as she opened the screen door and went out onto the screened porch.

A breathless Aaron met her at the bottom of the steps.

"Look what I found," he panted, proud of his discovery.

"Found?" Rachel questioned. "Didn't you catch it fishing?"

"Nope."

"Is it dead?" Rachel asked.

"Yeah." Aaron nodded his head, trying to slip the large fish from his underarm grip without dropping it. "It's dead all right, but in a funny sort of way."

"What do you mean, dead in a funny sort of way?" Rachel asked, staring at the fish, glad that at least it didn't look rotten.

Then, before he could answer, she realized she couldn't smell it; there was no fresh fish aroma at all and certainly nothing offensive, although she was within a few feet of the creature.

"Well, I mean it's so dead it's stiff," Aaron explained, sitting on the bottom step with the fish across his knees. "It doesn't feel like a fish should either, and it sure don't stink."

Rachel reached down and gingerly poked the big fish with her finger.

"You're right, and no wonder; the thing appears to have been preserved by a taxidermist."

"What's that?" the stocky little boy asked. "A taxi-what?"

"Taxidermist," Rachel repeated, laughing lightly. "A person who prepares fish and animals for display."

"Oh, you mean like in a museum," Aaron said, suddenly understanding.

"Exactly where did you find it, Aaron?" Rachel asked.

"In some bushes along the edge of the bluff where your property meets the old lane. Me and Holly were searching for arrowheads, but found this instead. What do you think we oughta do with it?"

"I really don't know. It's not bad looking. Matthew might like it on his study wall if you'd want to let him use it."

"Yeah, that's a good idea. Should we show it to Grandmama?" He got up, clutching the fish against his chest, and started up the steps.

Rachel held the screen door open for him, then the door from the kitchen.

"Hey, Grandmama," he called, his dark eyes twinkling; "want some fish for supper?"

Caroline turned from the sink, her mouth dropping open.

"You caught that in our river?" she asked, drying her hands on her apron.

"Naw, come look close at it." Aaron positioned the fish carefully on the seat of one of the chairs by the table.

"Well, I'll be!" she exclaimed, bending over to scrutinize and sniff at it. Then she picked it up by the tail.

"I've never seen one like this. It looks real, but feels artificial. There's no coolness or dampness like a raw fish—and no aroma."

"Rachel said a taxi-something must have fixed it. She said they fix animals this way for museums."

The light dawned on Rachel and Caroline simultaneously, because their eyes suddenly met and both exclaimed, "Of course, that's it!"

"What's it?" Aaron asked, puzzled.

"Didn't you hear talk about the hijacked truck that was found abandoned near here, son?" his grandmother asked. "It was carrying prepared specimens for the new nature museum to be opened soon in South Bend. This must be one of them."

"Why would anyone hijack a truck just to get something like this?" Aaron wondered aloud.

"They must have had what they thought was a good reason, because when they're caught, they'll probably face a prison sentence," Rachel told him.

"Wonder if they're armed and dangerous." He obviously relished the prospect of some excitement.

But that possibility sent a chill down Rachel's spine. She shivered, thinking it was very probable; and they, whoever *they* were, had been on her property within the last few days—or nights.

She dreaded the thought of someone skulking around while she slept.

I'll be glad when Matthew's settled in the carriage house, she thought. *Even though it's a good distance from here, it'll be comforting to know he's there.*

Aloud she said, "Aunt Caroline, would you mind staying over tonight?"

"I was about to suggest that myself, honey. You and I can do some extra baking to put in the freezer."

But even though she wasn't alone in the vast house, Rachel found herself peering cautiously out windows and drawing shades as dusk approached.

Chapter Nine

The following morning, Rachel and Tassie took Aunt Caroline's truck into Wedgewood with Aaron squeezed between them, the fish resting across his lap and Rachel's.

They trooped into the Police Chief's office and laid the fish on his desk, telling him their story. He thanked them effusively for this small break in the case that had everyone stumped.

After carefully questioning Aaron about his find, Chief Turner said, "We haven't been able to understand why the crooks abandoned the haul, leaving most of the truck's contents. Even has the museum perplexed; the stuff would be of little value to anyone else, except another museum or some guy's den or family room.

"Don't guess they could easily fence something like that, though," he concluded.

"Do you think the flooding that caused some roadblocks back then may have had anything to do with their decision to leave what they'd stolen?" Rachel questioned.

"Might have, at that; hadn't thought of it that way," the chief admitted.

"Hey, Joe, come in here; see what we've got," he called to a uniformed young man passing by the open door.

He addressed Aaron and the two young women. "You can go; I'll give you a call if we need to talk with you further."

"You did a fine job," he added, with a pleasant grin for Aaron. "Might be a little reward for you when we crack this case. If nothing else, I'll treat you to an ice cream sundae."

That afternoon Matthew called to let her know he'd arrived home and to confirm their supper date for the following evening.

"It'll be good to see you again, Rachel," he said softly before hanging up. "I've missed you very much."

The next evening Rachel was waiting on the front porch, ready to run out to the car when Matthew arrived. But she stepped back inside to remind Tassie that the Johnsons were to have the southwest bedroom, and just as she returned, the Archer car drove up the drive.

Before she reached the bottom step, the driver's door opened; Rachel was startled to see Matthew get out and begin walking toward her, using only a cane.

She stopped abruptly, watching his slow, somewhat jerky stride. Pausing only a moment she rushed forward to greet him, happiness overflowing her heart.

"Oh, Matthew, I'm so happy for you!" Rachel threw her arms around him.

"Whoa, there!" he laughed, staggering backward. "I'm still unsteady on this thing."

"I'm sorry!" she apologized, a bit embarrassed; then she laughed too and helped him steady himself.

"I was so shocked to see you get out of the car," Rachel explained as they settled in the car, fastening seat belts.

"That's the surprise you had for me?"

Matthew grinned. "Had a hard time not telling you over the phone. I'm just learning to get used to the prosthesis; but since it's the left leg, it doesn't interfere with my driving. You're not uncomfortable about it, are you?"

"No, I feel safe with you; though I could drive if you find it a problem later."

"Agreed," Matthew responded, "but I don't think it'll be necessary."

The clear summer evening offered a pleasant drive to Wedgewood. Red and gold streaks left by the setting sun blazed for a while, low on the western horizon, then became muted as dusk began to sift through the trees and float softly over the car.

"Smell the perfume of the evening, Matthew," Rachel said as she breathed deeply of the breeze coming through her open window. "I always notice the smell of flowers more at night than in the daytime, don't you?"

"Probably because there aren't as many distractions," Matthew nodded in agreement, stopping the car for traffic at a crossroad.

Even above the sound of the car, they could hear the sudden, sharp call of a hawk, and in the distance, the barking of dogs.

They could see the scattered lights of farmhouses now, and then soon the cluster of illumination that was Wedgewood.

Tinbell's supper menu was limited but satisfying. Rachel and Matthew relished thick hamburgers and piping hot fries, ending their meal with fresh strawberry banana splits.

While they were lingering over their ice cream, Rachel looked into Matthew's eyes. "It's a joy to see you so relaxed and in control of your life again, Matthew. I was so worried about you those first days following your surgery."

"You thought I wouldn't recover?"

"Oh, I knew you were getting along well enough physically; it was your state of mind that worried me."

"Guess I was a real mess for a while, Rachel; angry at everyone, even God."

"Well, there was that, too," Rachel agreed pensively, "but your silent times bothered me most."

"In what way?"

Rachel searched for words to express the anxiety she'd felt during those times.

"So often, after you'd lash out in anger, then apologize, it seemed like you were about to give up, Matthew. Like you didn't care what happened anymore."

Rachel paused, still grasping for a way to tell him what she'd felt.

Matthew listened attentively, his eyes on her face. Both of them had forgotten their dessert; the ice cream had melted into the strawberries, making pink marble swirls.

"I was afraid you were going to just spend your life sitting in that wheelchair," Rachel finally blurted emotionally.

Matthew gave a short, wry laugh.

"You read me correctly, Rachel. That's exactly the lousy

mood I'd get into sometimes. My attitude was rotten, and I knew it.

"But I couldn't seem to help myself from slipping into self-pity."

"What changed you?" she asked softly. "I remember your telling me Chaplain Bob was a big help to you."

"It was the Lord really, of course, but it was Bob who got me on the right track."

Matthew chuckled. "When I arrived at the Rehab Center, I was in one of those dark moods; stayed that way for several days feeling real sorry for myself.

"Then Bob took me in hand, and after learning I was a Christian, he gave me a stern talking to."

"What did he say?" Rachel asked, smiling.

"Told me I'd better shape up. That although God understood my natural human sense of doom, it wasn't what He wanted from a child of His."

"What did he think God *did* want from you?"

"He said the Lord wants the constant surrender to Him from His children, no matter what He permits to happen in their lives.

"But, at the same time," Matthew continued, "we're not to be resigned to circumstances in the sense of feeling helpless or without hope."

"What suggestions did the chaplain have for doing this?" Rachel asked.

"Bob told me that because God loves us, He's made a plan for each of our lives. I don't remember the verse, or where it's located in the Bible, but Bob quoted a verse that assures Christians that before they were born, even before they were formed, the plan for their lives was prepared."

"It's an awesome thought, isn't it?" Rachel remarked.

"Sure is; helps me see—just a bit—the sovereignty of God.

"Also helps me understand Bob's comment that resigning ourselves to circumstances and then inwardly fighting and resenting them will only make us miserable. And I know for sure that it does."

"I had to learn that, too," Rachel admitted. "Only in a much smaller way, and for a less serious reason."

"I guess how enormous the situation seems isn't what matters," Matthew said. "The important thing is that we truly want His will for our lives, whether it seems to fit our present plans or not."

Rachel nodded. "I'm glad we're both learning that lesson; glad we've each accepted God's loving plans for us. I want to continue to trust the Lord to guide me—I hope I do."

"We can only ask God to help us with that," Matthew said, picking up his spoon and dipping into the strawberry sauce and cream.

When they walked out to the car, a half moon had risen, bathing the gravelly parking lot with a soft glow.

Gazing up at the sky with the red-and-blue neon sign of Tinbell's at their back, they could see hundreds of stars beginning to prick the cloudless evening sky.

"Isn't it beautiful, Matthew? I'm always especially thankful for my eyesight when I see something like this."

"Me, too, Rachel," Matthew said quietly, slipping his arm easily around her shoulders.

They stood together in silence for a few minutes, enjoying the glorious sky. Rachel silently thanked God for the deep sense of caring friendship they shared.

When she turned her head to look up at him, Rachel found him watching her intently, the soft light of the moon reflected in his eyes, his face disconcertingly close.

She was glad for the darkness that concealed the blush she felt touch her cheek, as her heart was touched with an extra warmth for this young man who was becoming more than a friend.

A small group of chatting, laughing people exiting Tinbell's jarred them back to the reality of the moment. Leaving his arm around her shoulder, Matthew guided her to his car.

Aware of his still shaky gait, Rachel wondered if walking was painful for him.

"Does your leg hurt, Matthew?" she asked.

"Some," he admitted as they reached the car and he unlocked her door.

"I've not had it long enough to become hardened to it.

"It'll take a while, but it's great to be walking, even with the discomfort."

The drive back to Mulberry Inn was even more pleasant than the trip in to Wedgewood earlier. After leaving the lights of the little town, they could see that thousands more stars had become visible. The Milky Way appeared like a filmy, luminous chiffon scarf swirled across the heavens.

When they reached the inn and Matthew had walked with her to the bottom of the steps leading to the veranda, he leaned against the newel post and slipped the curve of his cane over the handrail.

"Thank you for a lovely evening, Matthew," Rachel began.

He put an arm around her shoulders, as he'd done earlier. But instead of gazing at the panorama of the sky, he lifted his hand and put a finger under her chin, gently tipping her head.

Although she could see his face only dimly in the faint light from the doorside lantern above them, Rachel sensed, rather than saw, the affection in his eyes.

She couldn't have averted her gaze even if she had wanted to, because Matthew's finger gently, but firmly, held her face tilted toward his.

Very slowly he bent his head. Kissing her softly on the forehead, his voice was quiet, filled with tenderness. "You're becoming very important to me, Rachel. Every day I find you filling more and more of my thoughts."

Then suddenly, gently, he dropped his hand and slipped his arm from her shoulders.

Turning a bit awkwardly, he retrieved his cane and, with a soft "Good night, honey," he headed through the deepening dusk toward the car with his uneven gait.

A faint, sweet aroma reached Rachel from the soft breeze moving over a flowerbed nearby. She smiled dreamily, thinking, "I'll always remember this special night with Matthew when I smell the perfume of yellow roses."

Chapter Ten

During the last days of August, Mrs. Archer and a friend moved furniture and appliances into the carriage house. Matthew's personal belongings were brought in, and Mrs. Archer and Rachel scurried around, making sure every detail in the refurbished cottage was ready for his arrival.

Matthew's mother stocked the refrigerator and cupboards as her last loving chore, and was just leaving when Rachel arrived with a loaf of fresh bread and a plate of cookies.

"How nice, dear," Mrs. Archer smiled, getting into her car. "I see I won't have to be concerned about Matthew fending for himself while still getting used to his new leg."

Rachel laughed lightly. "Aunt Caroline has plans for all sorts of things she's going to make for him, even though he assured her he's a passable cook. Is he still planning to be in his new home tonight?"

"Yes, we're having dinner in town with old family friends, since my husband and I will be leaving Wedgewood day after tomorrow. We'll bring Matthew here around ten tonight.

"Again, thank you so much for your help and for making the cottage available, Rachel," she added just before starting her car.

"Mrs. Archer, would you and Mr. Archer have tomorrow evening free to come here for dinner? I would love to have a last visit before you move."

"Yes, we're free; that sounds delightful." Mrs. Archer backed the car into the turnaround in front of the cottage.

"Good. I'll leave a note on the table with these baked goods, telling Matthew he's invited," Rachel called after her.

Rachel gladly accepted Aunt Caroline's offer to cook the

farewell dinner, made when she phoned to invite her to join them for the evening.

"I'll enjoy preparing the meal," she told Rachel the next morning when she arrived. "I just won't join you. I love that boy dearly, but he should have that last night with his folks and you."

Aunt Caroline's eyes twinkled as she continued. "I'm beginning to think that family is quite taken with you—Matthew especially."

Rachel blushed a little, nodding her head with a smile before turning toward the dining room.

From a wide drawer in the buffet she took a heavy linen tablecloth and four matching napkins.

Draping the table with care, Rachel placed squat silver candlesticks at each end, then went to the china cabinet where she carefully removed delicate Spode pieces.

When she'd finished setting the table with shining silver flatware, Rachel stepped back to admire her handiwork.

"Pretty, isn't it?" Aunt Caroline said from the kitchen doorway. "Your Aunt Esther had a silver bowl behind one of the buffet doors. It'd be beautiful in the middle of your table filled with some of those late roses at the front of the house."

"Thanks, Aunt Caroline," Rachel beamed. "That's exactly the finishing touch it needs."

That evening in the candle-lit dining room, Rachel and the Archers enjoyed a sense of deep fellowship, along with their fried chicken dinner that began with a chilled fruit soup and ended with fresh peach pie.

Before retiring late that night, Rachel stood at her open upstairs bedroom window brushing her hair.

In the distance, beyond the barn, she caught the glint of moonlight on moving water, where the river curved toward Wedgewood.

Halfway between the barn area and the inn, a small light gleamed from the carriage house nestled among the sycamore trees.

Rachel smiled softly, a contented feeling in her heart, knowing she'd had a part in making a home for Matthew, her dear friend.

The sudden quickening of her heartbeat made her admit to herself that he was becoming more than a special friend.

She considered that a while, wondering if it was what she wanted.

Matthew's certainly a man who's earned my respect, she mused, thinking about his physical perseverance and change of attitude since his accident.

He's intelligent as well as fun to be with; best of all, and most important, he's a Christian and wants God to lead him in the decisions in his life.

But even with all those things going for him that make him a fellow any girl could be proud of, is he the one I want to get serious about?

Rachel sighed, then mumbled to herself, "Be honest, Rachel; what you really mean is, do I want to get serious about a guy who's crippled, who will be handicapped to some extent for the rest of his life?"

A bit ashamed of herself, yet wanting to be realistic, Rachel knew she didn't have the answer to that question.

After a last glance at the lovely moon-lit sky and Matthew's light, she crossed the room to kneel beside her bed.

"Heavenly Father," she began hesitantly, "Matthew is beginning to mean a lot to me, but I'm confused about my real feelings toward him. Please help me understand what this relationship is to be in your plan for my life. I really do want your will. Amen."

Stretching out on the cool sheet of her bed, Rachel's thoughts turned to the trespassers that had been on her property, the stolen truck abandoned nearby, and the intense gaze of the stranger in the park during the Fourth of July fair. And she thought of Matthew.

Rachel turned onto her side, curling herself slightly, ready for sleep.

I'm fairly sure I'm safe here, she thought drowsily, *but it's nice to know someone is near I can depend on if I need help.*

September brought purple asters, goldenrod, black-eyed Susan's and flocks of cawing crows. But the weeks passed quickly. Rachel kept busy helping Aunt Caroline freeze and can vegetables from her large garden and fruit from Rachel's orchard on the inn's land.

An increase of autumn tourists driving through the scenic area, many of whom took advantage of Mulberry Inn's hospitality, also demanded daily attention to rooms and mounds of laundry.

Rachel dropped into bed late each night, completely exhausted, but with a fine sense of accomplishment.

September slipped away, the nights became cooler, and bright green leaves on the trees turned almost overnight to yellows and reds.

Matthew was back at the Center for a couple of weeks. Rachel missed his cheerful presence, as he had usually puttered around the grounds each evening.

"I'd like to do as much of the yard work for you as I can," he'd said. "As a thanks for being able to live in such a nice place instead of a room in town. It'll help me get more used to my leg, too.

"Sitting in a chair in the bank's loan department gets tiring, so working outdoors is a pleasure."

After the explanation, Rachel welcomed his help without feeling she might be taking advantage of his generous nature.

She wished he were here now to enjoy with her the trees dressed in riots of blazing color against the green of spruce and pine, and the bright blue of the sky.

She missed, too, their weekly dates at Tinbell's and the suppers he occasionally shared with her in the inn's kitchen while tourist guests chatted over dessert and coffee in the parlor.

The days until his return seemed to crawl by, although she was occupied with picking and storing late apples, and twice helping Aunt Caroline bring in squash and pumpkins from the garden at the Wolcott home.

Rachel found each time that some of them had been placed in the back of the truck. When she returned from work in Wedgewood, Tassie drove her back to the inn, and the two girls carried them to the back porch.

"I'll bring Aaron over after school Friday or Saturday," Tassie said the day they finished. "He can lug them out to the root cellar for you."

Saturday, after Aaron finished the job, except for one pumpkin, he suggested, "This sure would make a great jack-o'-lantern for your front porch, Rachel. How about if I carve it for you?"

"I'd like that, Aaron," she smiled. "I haven't made one for years; it used to be lots of fun."

"Wanna help?" Aaron offered.

"No," Rachel laughed. "Your imagination and carving will make a much better one than I could."

"You got an extra candle I can have for it?" Aaron asked hopefully.

"Sure have," Rachel answered. "I'll put in on the back porch for you."

She and Tassie had been in the backyard cutting mums and sprays of airy baby's-breath to prepare room bouquets for the two families expected that evening.

"Let's have a cup of tea while Aaron carves the pumpkin," Rachel suggested. Then she called to him, "Come in for milk and cookies when you're finished, Aaron."

After arranging the flowers and taking them upstairs, the girls returned to the kitchen and the pot of steeping aromatic tea.

"I have some iced tea in the refrigerator if you'd prefer that, Tassie," Rachel offered, bringing the pot and two mugs with pink sprigs painted on them to the table.

Tassie shook her head and Rachel said, "I remember these mugs from when I was a little girl; Aunt Esther always served hot chocolate in one for me."

"You have good memories of this place to add to the enjoyment of living here, don't you?" Tassie commented.

"I was here only a few times in my childhood, but they were fun times," Rachel said as she sipped her tea thoughtfully.

Tassie smiled. "I remember being here once when I was little; about Aaron's age, I think. Not here in the house, but in the barn.

"Aunt Esther and Mama had a Halloween party for the youngsters at the church."

"That sounds like fun!" Rachel exclaimed. "Do you think we'd have time to get something like that together? We'd have almost two weeks."

"Are you sure you want to bother?" Tassie asked. "You've been so busy lately."

"Oh, the rush is over now," Rachel assured her. "I had no guests at all last week and only two the week before. Let's plan a party! It could be fun."

"Will you want to have it in your barn?" Tassie questioned.

"That seems like the best place, although it's quite a distance from the house and we'd have to carry everything out there. But, there may be a wheelbarrow or something stored in there that we could use."

"How about using the truck?" Tassie suggested.

"There's a barrier of posts sunk into the ground across the lane that leads out there," Rachel explained. "Probably used as carstops for extra parking spaces at some time."

"Couldn't I drive around them?"

"I doubt it. Trees and bushes grow up rather close there, if I remember right," Rachel answered. "I've been over that way only once. That lane leads out around the south edge of the yard and continues on not too far from the dead-end one on the next property, where the hijacked truck was found abandoned a few months ago.

"The drive around the north of the house goes to the carriage house, though I always take a shortcut through the backyard and that little field."

"Anyway, let's go check the barn for possibilities, shall we?" Rachel stood up to pour a tall glass of milk for Aaron.

He was sitting against a tree not far from the back steps absorbed in carving a leering face in the round orange pumpkin.

"Cookies and milk are on the table, Aaron," Rachel called as they passed nearby.

"Okay," he grinned, looking up. "Where you goin'?"

"Out to the barn," Tassie answered. "Maybe going to plan a harvest party."

"Why did you call it a harvest party instead of Halloween?" Rachel asked. "Don't you want a masquerade and scary things for the kids? They're what add the fun and excitement."

"Well, sure, the masquerade's okay . . ." Tassie said; "that makes the party. But some folks have reservations about Halloween because of its connections with pagan superstitions and the occult at times. So the folks at church who usually plan the parties call them harvest parties instead."

"That makes sense," Rachel agreed. "We'll definitely make the invitations for a harvest party then."

The two girls strolled along the old unused lane, their feet scattering the accumulation of already fallen leaves, chatting happily about plans for the party, and laughing lightly over their suggestions for the scary things that youngsters delight in being frightened by momentarily.

Bare-branched trees revealed long-abandoned bird nests; the air was crisp, making sweaters welcome.

Approaching the barn, they found the area badly overgrown, and the space before the big door a tangle of briars and waist-high weeds.

"Doesn't look like we'll get in there very easily," Tassie mumbled.

Rachel took several steps off the lane into some brushy grass and weeds, craning her neck.

"Looks like a door around the corner; let's check it," she said.

"Be just our luck to find it locked," Tassie grumbled.

"Don't be so pessimistic," Rachel laughed, heading on through the heavy growth, stopping a moment to gaze upward in awe at the aerial flight of a large buzzard—poetry in motion.

Tassie stood where she was until Rachel reached the door, tried it, and called, "You were right, Tassie; it's locked. I'll ask Matthew to look it over for us. He's due back Monday, and will probably want to get in on these plans."

"Aaron will be excited to hear that," Tassie laughed as Rachel came back through the weeds and tall pole-like horsetail stalks. "He thinks Matthew's a very special guy."

"I do, too," Rachel admitted, smiling.

"Thought you did," Tassie's eyes twinkled. "It shows sometimes, you know."

Chapter Eleven

Matthew arrived just before noon the next day, stopping at the inn to say hello to Rachel before driving back to his cottage.

"Stay for lunch, Matthew," she invited. "Unless you'd rather have hot coffee, there's cold lemonade ready and I'll make sandwiches."

"Can't pass up an invitation like that," he responded. "In fact," he added, grinning, "I sort of hoped you'd invite me."

While she sliced bread and cold beef roast, he sat at the table telling her about the things he'd been doing to try to strengthen his leg.

"I wondered why I couldn't seem to regain strength as fast as I expected to, but had decided maybe that's just the way it is in cases like this," he explained.

"Doc Jenkins seemed concerned at times because of some of the pain, but decided I probably just needed a change in my therapy routine."

"Did that help?" Rachel asked.

"Seems to be relieving it."

Then he noticed the jack-o'-lantern on the counter. "Looks like you've been doing some pretty fancy carving."

Rachel laughed. "That's Aaron's handiwork. He thinks I should have it on the front porch to greet guests, but I told him I'd rather save it for the party."

"What party?"

"The harvest party we're planning at Halloween time. I told Tassie you'd help me check out the barn to see if it's an okay spot. She said her mom and Aunt Esther held one years ago

112

for a bunch of kids, but I have no idea what condition the barn's in now."

"Sure, I'll help you. Want to do it this evening, or late this afternoon after I get back from the bank? I told them I'd come in for a few hours today."

"Anytime is fine," Rachel said. "You can phone this afternoon and let me know for sure. If you're tired after your trip, the barn could wait until tomorrow evening."

"Think I'll take you up on that idea," Matthew said. "I'll meet you in your backyard around four-thirty tomorrow. After we've checked out the barn, we'll drive in to Tinbell's for supper, okay?"

"That'll be nice, Matthew. I've missed you and our times together," she said as they carried their lunch out to the picnic table under the oak tree.

Brown leaves occasionally drifted down onto the table as they discussed ideas for entertaining the young people who would be invited to the party. Matthew swallowed a bite of his sandwich. "Too bad some of the summer residents aren't still here. It would mean some extra kids in that age group."

"I think there may be at least one," Rachel answered. "Aaron said the Kiepuras were to be down that weekend to close up their cottage—turn off the water and things like that to prepare it for winter.

"Mrs. Kiepura told him they might bring Michael along. If they do, Aaron's going to invite him. But he's mainly excited about their coming because of Holly."

"You mean their dog? What about her?" Matthew asked.

"The Kiepuras plan to spend the winter with someone in Wisconsin. They're leaving Ginger, the doberman, with their grandsons, but Aaron pestered them to let Holly stay with him," Rachel laughed. "They finally gave in to him. They know he'll take good care of her."

The next morning, although part of the attic still needed to be gone through, the out-of-doors beckoned to Rachel.

Irresistibly drawn to the lovely autumn landscape, Rachel hurriedly slipped into her jeans and jacket, wrapped two raisin muffins in a paper napkin, and put them and an apple in her pocket.

Filling a small thermos with orange juice, she slipped it into the other jacket pocket and took a pair of binoculars from a hook just inside the pantry, where she'd found them a few weeks earlier.

"Your Aunt Esther was quite a bird-watcher before she became so feeble," Aunt Caroline had told her. "Believe she kept binoculars upstairs, too, so they'd always be handy if she happened to notice something interesting out a window."

Rachel slipped the strap around her neck, closed the kitchen door behind her, and picked up a small basket as she crossed the back porch.

A squirrel in the big oak tree scolded her sharply when she passed beneath him; she chuckled at his antics.

The crisp, cold air tinged her cheeks and the tip of her nose a healthy pink.

Rachel's hair bounced softly against her shoulders as she walked briskly across the yard, skirted the root-cellar mound and went through the gate in the rail fence.

Instead of following the path that led to the left and eventually to the carriage house, she angled off to the right, toward one of the areas of the bluff above the river she hadn't yet visited.

Breathing deeply of the clear air, Rachel stood among frost-browned ferns and Virginia creeper and gazed at the swiftly moving stream below. In the bright sunshine of this vibrant day, the night she and Tassie had been caught beneath those waters in the truck seemed long ago.

Scuffing though the leaves, she continued along the bluff to the right, coming finally to the concrete stairs leading down to the river's edge.

The water's much lower than during the high-water period last spring, she thought. *But I should remember to warn the kids at the party to not go down there.*

Rachel went farther down the steps to sit on the stone bench and scan the far bank with her binoculars. She focused on a group of migrating ducks that had just landed among some rushes.

A large turtle slipped off a rock in the water just below her, causing a small splash. Her glasses found him and continued along her side of the river to directly below where, she thought, the old barn was located.

A small animal was paddling around in the water near the shore, and Rachel adjusted the binoculars in order to see him more clearly.

"Must be a muskrat," she decided as it moved into the brush at the water's edge.

Just beyond that spot, something caught her eye, a glint of metal touched by the sun.

Unable to figure out what it was, Rachel mused, *Aaron probably forgot his little tin-can submarine the last time he played down there.*

Then she laughed softly. "He must have felt ambitious; looks like he cleared a path through the brush up the hillside. Would have worn me out."

Rachel watched a woodpecker industriously searching a tree trunk for insects. Before getting up from the bench, she gave a lingering look toward the river glistening in the sunshine. The ducks lifted off the water, circling, then headed south, and she observed the magnificent beauty of the colors surrounding her.

Climbing the steps up the hill, she skipped a bit as she went, exulting in being alive, in being able to see and hear clearly, in having the ability to easily walk and run.

At that thought, the remembrance of Matthew's uneven gait slowed her step. She wondered if he would ever be able to walk normally again.

"May he regain needed strength, Lord," she prayed quietly, as she reached the top of the bluff. "Help him learn to walk correctly and without pain. He loves you, and I do, too. Teach us your will for our lives."

On her stroll back to the house, Rachel filled her basket to overflowing with colorful leaves and the snowflake-like "umbrellas" of queen-anne's lace, each one centered with a scarlet dot, like a tiny drop of blood.

From the wisteria vine on the rail fence, she plucked long brown seed pods and a few tendrils.

Back in the house, she collected a few crockery pitchers

from the pantry and arranged her treasures from nature in them.

"I'll enjoy them in here, then put them on the refreshment tables in the barn Friday," she decided.

Shortly after four o'clock that afternoon, Rachel was waiting for Matthew. She had heard his car on the drive about an hour before, so she knew he'd returned from the bank.

I can hardly wait to see him, even though I was just with him yesterday, she thought.

The sound of a car's motor told her Matthew had arrived.

He's here early just like I am, Rachel smiled, going to greet him. *Maybe he's as eager to see me as I am to see him*, she hoped.

Slowing the car to a stop near her, and getting out, Matthew thought, *She mirrors the beautiful colors around her*. He took in the green and gold plaid shirt and the bit of yellow sweater visible between her lapels. His gaze lingered on the long, flowing blonde hair resting over the shoulders of her bronze-colored jacket.

She's absolutely lovely, Matthew reflected, reaching out to take her hand.

"Now for the barn," he announced. "Did you find the key?"

"I found several on a key ring hanging in the pantry. I'm hoping one of them fits," Rachel held them up and jingled them before slipping them back into her jacket pocket.

"Matthew, are you going to be able to make the walk out there all right?"

"I expect so, but we won't know until I give it a try, so let's go."

He grinned. "That steak supper is waiting for us, too, don't forget."

Rachel's hand was clasped firmly in Matthew's strong one as they walked along the lane, their feet crunching crisp leaves and clumps of weeds growing in their path.

"I'll ask Aaron if he can get a friend to help him cut some of these," he offered.

"They're much worse around the barn," she said. "I'd like to have the big doors open for the party, but there's a tangle of tall things growing in front of them."

"Several of the older boys at the church will probably help out," Matthew suggested. "I'll give them a call tonight; see if they can stop by after school tomorrow."

"I'd appreciate that," Rachel affirmed. "I hope there's something in the barn to cut them with."

"Dad left his gas-powered weed cutter for the church custodian—we'll borrow that. It'll make fast work of the job."

"We may be able to get this together in a few days, after all," Rachel smiled.

When they reached the barn, Rachel found, with relief, that the largest of the keys on the ring fit the old lock. Standing knee-deep in weeds, Rachel make several attempts before it turned, grating as she forced it.

Matthew was beside her now and, reaching over her shoulder, helped her push the stubborn door open.

Bits of dust and gritty dirt showered down from cracks over the doorway dislodged by the sudden jarring of the door. Rachel stepped aside just in time to avoid it.

"Maybe we shouldn't have planned to do this before going into town," she laughed. "I may be a mess by then."

"Let me go ahead," Matthew offered. "My short hair will brush out more easily than yours if that happens again."

Rachel willingly stepped aside, following him into the cavernous building. Surprisingly, it didn't smell as musty as she'd expected.

The soft cooing of doves came to them. Looking up, they saw them lined side by side on a rafter near a small wood-shuttered window. The shutters hung by one hinge, providing an entrance for them.

"Looks like they've found their roosting spot for the winter," Matthew commented, "but I'll bet the kids would prefer bats for the party."

"No doubt," Rachel laughed, "but I'll take the doves, thank you."

Slanting rays of the early setting sun reached through a barn window revealing a wall hung with old-time tools, a large crosscut saw and a long-handled scythe.

The wood floor echoed their steps and the slight thump of Matthew's cane as they walked over to the partially lit area to inspect an old pot-belly stove.

Next to it on an old table were pottery crocks and jugs of various sizes, their glazed surfaces dulled by dust. Nearby sat an iron cookstove, its top cluttered with heavy, black iron pots and skillets.

"With these and the things in the attic, I could open an antique store," Rachel laughed, only half joking.

"Not a bad idea," Matthew agreed. "Even better would be a comfortable 'when Grandpa was a boy' type of place where young people could hang out."

Stopping abruptly in her tracks, Rachel forgot about heading to the other corner where she'd spotted some wagon wheels leaning against the wall next to a copper wash boiler.

She was quiet several minutes, lost in thought, turning Matthew's unexpected suggestion over in her mind.

Finally becoming aware of the cooing of the doves, of Matthew's, "Rachel?" and his touch on her arm, Rachel turned to him, smiling. "Matthew, that's a marvelous idea; it would be perfect. Kids could come for fun or to talk about their problems; we'd have refreshments for them—and games—someone could—"

"Hey, wait, Rachel," Matthew chuckled. "I didn't know I was going to unleash an avalanche of plans and extra work for you."

"It wouldn't seem like work, Matthew!" she exclaimed. "You'd help me, wouldn't you?"

"Sure, but something like that's not as simple as it seems at first glance. We'll talk about it."

"Okay." Rachel shook her head, laughing a bit at herself. "Guess I did get over-enthusiastic for a minute."

"I'm glad you're that way. At least you're willing to try something new, and I do think this may be the start of a great idea!"

"Oh, I hope so," Rachel said eagerly. "I'd love to see this idea turn out to be something wonderful!"

Matthew took her hand, leading her to another dilapidated table against the far wall. "Thought these looked like decoys," he said, picking up one that was obviously supposed to be a mallard drake.

"This is a nice collection," he commented, blowing the dust from a wood pintail.

"We'll never be able to get all this stuff moved and the place cleaned by Friday evening." Rachel's voice betrayed the beginnings of discouragement. "And I'll need time to make sandwiches and bake some desserts."

"We'll ask a few of the young people's mothers to help out with the food this time," Matthew decided, turning to leave the barn, still holding her hand.

"As for this place, I like it the way it is. We'll dust off the surfaces of the stoves and tables, but the rest can add to the harvest atmosphere."

"You're right," Rachel agreed with relief. "Those cobwebs draped all over should be okay." A soft, questioning "meow" reached their ears just before a large black cat emerged from the bushes.

"He'll be a great party addition, too," Rachel laughed.

"He's also the reason we didn't see any mice scurrying around in there. I wondered about that," Matthew chuckled.

They locked the door behind them, turning to enjoy the glowing red and gold streaks on the western horizon before returning to the car.

"Would you mind a short detour before dinner?" Matthew inquired. "As long as we're going in that general direction, I'd like to go by Maple Grove and pick up some cider."

"Sounds like a delicious detour," Rachel smiled.

They drove through the countryside in a blend of early dusk and lingering daylight.

Choruses of cricket and locust songs reached their ears when they slowed for the lane at the little cider mill, and stopped at the edge of a small grove of apple trees.

Beneath a large tree in the center of a small clearing at the edge of the grove, an elderly man bent over his work in the final rays of rose-tinged daylight. Looking up, he hollered, "Howdy, Matt, good to see ya. C'mon over."

Rachel and Matthew walked toward him through thick, sweet-smelling grass just beginning to lose its bright summer green.

"Ummm," Rachel murmured as the sharp, sweet aroma of

freshly squeezed apples assailed her nostrils.

"Mr. Kimbro, this is Rachel Hoekstra, Esther Simon's grandniece. She owns Mulberry Inn now."

"Right smart glad to meet you, Miss Hoekstra," the genial old gentleman said, clasping her offered hand with his work-worn one.

"Glad you phoned you were comin', Matt," he said, turning to shake his hand. "Was about to close up for the day and go in to fix me a bit of supper."

"Better give me four gallons, Mr. Kimbro," Matthew said. "We're planning a harvest party for some young people."

Mr. Kimbro chuckled as he began filling a glass jug from a large wood barrel on a platform.

"Many's the apple I've bobbed for and the gals I spooked in times past."

When the jugs were filled, he glanced up into the branches of the large maple tree towering over his little cider press. "Pretty, ain't it? Still holding its color; it's the last one to lose its leaves every year. I hate to see winter coming, but that fella always helps autumn last a bit longer.

"Well, mustn't keep you young folks; enjoy your evening and the party coming up."

"Mr. Kimbro," Matthew spoke impulsively, "how about enjoying the evening with us? We're going in to Tinbell's for supper."

Glancing toward Rachel to see if she agreed, Matthew continued. "We'd like you to be our guest; how about it?"

Taken aback at the unexpected invitation, the old gentleman looked from one to the other, wiping his palms against his overalls.

"Please do, Mr. Kimbro," Rachel urged sincerely, reaching out to touch his red plaid shirtsleeve.

"I'd need to freshen up," he said after a moment, "but, yes, I'd like to do that."

"You go on and get ready," Matthew suggested. "We'll put the cider in the car and pick you up at the house shortly."

Sending a happy grin their way, Mr. Kimbro bustled off toward the ancient white farmhouse.

"That was a nice thing to do, Matthew," Rachel said, picking up a jug of the clear, amber liquid.

"He's a fine old gentleman," Matthew answered. He hoisted a jug, then carefully balanced himself with the lopsided weight before heading to the car.

"I've been coming here for cider every autumn since I can remember. Dad always brought me along."

Matthew chuckled. "Mr. Kimbro always insisted I have a sample before he filled our jug, as though my opinion of his product had special value. He knew how to make children feel important."

"Now you do it," Rachel said. "I've noticed how you treat Aaron."

"I try to," Matthew answered, smiling at her through the dusk that had suddenly eclipsed the remaining daylight. "It's a steppingstone to explaining each person's importance to God."

Rachel thought about that while they went for the remaining cider jugs.

"I suppose it must be difficult for people who've been pushed into the background, and shown little love as children. I mean, to accept the fact that God loved them enough to send Jesus to the earth to die for them," she explained.

"Fortunately," Matthew continued, "whatever our background, that truth is a powerful piece of information."

After they were in the car driving up to the Kimbro house, he added, "If you follow through on the idea of turning the barn into a youth spot, I think it'll help in sharing that message."

The following day was spent clearing brush from around the barn and preparing the main interior for the party. Rachel knew the door near where the copper wash boiler stood probably led to extra space, perhaps stalls and such, but she was too busy to investigate.

This area ought to be enough for this time, she thought as she swept the wide plank floor and shoved bales of hay into position against the walls for seating.

Sure glad Matthew thought to have these sent over, she mused, puffing a bit as she maneuvered the last two.

Rachel wrinkled her nose, sniffing the sweet aroma of the

pile of fresh hay that had been dumped into the center of the large room. The kids would kneel there—around the big metal washtub of water—to bob for apples.

Aunt Caroline had arrived shortly after breakfast and her phone call.

"Tassie told me about the party; I'm coming over. I know you can use some extra help and she won't be off work till late afternoon. Aaron's coming after school for whatever you need him to do."

When Rachel returned to the house from the barn, she said, "I'll have Aaron carve some more jack-o'-lanterns. I have only one, and lots of them will be more festive."

"Aaron said he hopes you have lots of ghosts and other scary things," Aunt Caroline laughed. "He's been busy making a clown costume, which is just the opposite of scary."

"We're going to go easy on the scary stuff," Rachel said, smiling. "Matthew's going to help me hang some sheet-goblins and scarecrows from tree limbs around the barn, but that's about it."

"The kids will love this party," Aunt Caroline chuckled as she opened the oven door.

A luscious aroma of apples and cinnamon and nutmeg filled the kitchen.

"It'll be a trial, waiting till tomorrow night to taste those," Rachel said with appreciation.

"Let's not." Aunt Caroline's eyes twinkled as she slipped juicy pies onto cooling racks.

"I made an extra one just for sampling. We'll have it for our lunch, if that's all right with you."

"How about eating at eleven o'clock instead of noon?" Rachel said, in complete agreement with the menu.

Friday evening turned out to be perfect for the harvest party. Cool enough to make the young people comfortable in heavy sweaters, the breeze was just strong enough to make the draped sheets and scarecrows move back and forth.

As dusk fell, two dozen or so young people trooped up the lane to the huge barn, its dark form looming against the still-streaked sky. The wide-open double doors revealed glowing jack-o'-lanterns and tables loaded with goodies. Dressed like Abraham Lincoln, Matthew sat on a hay bale ready to oversee games.

Later, stars were pricking the blackness and a sliver of moon rode high in the sky. The air was filled with shrieks and laughter, while clowns and sparkly gowned ladies, a bear and a rotund Humpty Dumpty, the Lone Ranger and a cook in a tall white hat stumbled around the outside of the barn on a scavenger hunt.

When the cider jugs were empty, the last donut and piece of pie had disappeared, and the final package presented from the prize basket, "thank you's" and shouts of "goodbye" were exchanged as kids filled the cars of parents who had come for them.

Tassie and her boyfriend had gone on ahead to place one of the jack-o'-lanterns in the truck for Aaron. Candles were carefully snuffed out, and the barn doors were secured before Matthew and Aaron escorted Rachel up the lane toward the house.

"What part of the party did you enjoy most, Aaron?" Rachel asked, pointing the beam from her flashlight toward the edge of the lane so it wouldn't glare in his eyes.

"Well, the food was terrific," Aaron answered, twirling around, the light from his flashlight skimming over bushes and tree trunks.

"But the best thing of all was the dead guy. He was great!"

"The what?" Rachel asked, perplexed.

"That scarecrow; the hat and suit you stuffed to look like a dead man lying out back of the barn," he persisted, continuing his skipping twirl.

"Are you kidding us, Aaron?" Matthew asked.

"Naw, why would I do that? It was a terrific scare; all the kids said so. Those dumb girls screamed and ran, but I knew it was just for fun.

"But the dead guy sure looked real. I almost had too many chills up my own spine to go over and take a better look.

"Made that Betty Benson think I was really brave," he chuckled, standing still in the middle of the lane, laughingly seeking their approval.

Matthew and Rachel had stopped walking, too, and she

slipped her hand in his, shivering a little.

"Aaron," Matthew said sternly, "you're honestly not conning us?"

"Nope," the little boy answered, confused over the seriousness concerning one of their own inventions.

"Okay, then run on ahead," Matthew said, his voice more gentle.

Matthew tightened his grip on Rachel's hand; their eyes met in the distorting illumination from their flashlight.

"I believe we'd best just go straight to the house," he declared, his voice sounding hollow and strange. "I'll call the police and wait with you."

Chapter Twelve

Rachel and Matthew thanked Tassie and her friend, Todd Fletcher, for helping with the party. Waving goodbye to Aaron they waited impatiently while Todd's car made a U-turn out of the drive.

"Rachel, I think I'd better make *sure* there's a dead man here before I phone the police; Aaron could have been mistaken," Matthew suggested.

"But we didn't put anything on the other side of the barn," Rachel insisted. "I didn't even bother cutting the weeds there, because I didn't want the kids on the side toward the river.

"I realize the water's low now and they probably wouldn't have gone down there anyway at night, but I've been extra sensitive about the danger of the stream after my accident in the truck."

"Think I'll check anyway; one of the older teens may have brought his own addition to the party. I'd feel awfully foolish bringing the police all the way out here to investigate some kind of mannequin."

"I suppose you're right," Rachel admitted, wishing he weren't. She didn't want to go out there to check, but she didn't want him to go alone, either.

"Couldn't we wait till morning when it would be easier to get out there?" she asked hopefully.

"If there really is a man there, he could be injured, instead of dead. I need to make sure either way," he replied.

"Okay, but I'm going with you." Rachel reached for his hand.

"You don't have to, you know . . ."

"I want to, Matthew. I'd rather be with you finding a dead

man than to be here alone if a murderer is around."

"Come on, then." Matthew clasped her hand in a firmer grip.

The only sound as they retraced their steps back down the lane to the barn was the crunch of their footsteps on dry leaves and the soft sound of Matthew's cane tapping.

When they reached the barn, its dark form looming before them against the starry sky, they cut around to the left where some of the weeds had been cleared to make a path to the door several days before.

Rachel jumped as an owl hooted softly, but suddenly, from a large oak tree nearby.

Matthew answered with a soft squeeze of her hand.

"As I remember, there's a real tangle of weeds back there— probably full of burrs. Sure you want to go the rest of the way?"

"Yes," Rachel decided, tightly gripping the large flashlight that illuminated their way, picking out an area where the young people walking around had trampled the tall weeds in spots.

"Should be easier walking over this way." She slipped her hand from his to lead the way.

The weedy grass swished and crackled as she make her way around the corner to the back side of the large structure.

She had made herself tread about halfway alongside the length of the wall when the beam of her light picked it—him— out!

Rachel stopped abruptly, her breath drawing in with a gasp.

Coming up beside her, Matthew saw the figure sprawled face down among the weeds and slipped his arm around her shoulders.

"Does seem real all right, doesn't he?" Matthew commented.

"Too real . . ." Rachel answered, with a slight shiver.

"We'll have to make sure, you know," he said.

"I know, and you can't kneel down to check; right?"

"Right. It'll have to be up to you . . . I'm sorry."

Rachel handed the flashlight to Matthew, and they walked forward together to the silent figure of a man, dressed in a dark brown suit. He was lying like a discarded doll flung down in the tall grass and weeds.

Matthew stood close to the body, angling the flashlight's beam to shine fully on the head and suitcoat.

Hesitating a bit, Rachel looked imploringly at Matthew. Then, realizing he couldn't see her face in the darkness and was focusing his attention on the matter at hand, she slowly dropped to one knee and gingerly put out a hand to touch the side of the figure's face.

With a short cry, she quickly withdrew her hand.

"It's flesh; it's a real man," she affirmed quietly, looking up at Matthew.

"See whether he has a pulse," Matthew answered quickly.

Carefully fingering the wrist on the man's outflung arm, Rachel searched carefully, then shook her head.

"Try the pulse spot at the side of the neck," Matthew instructed.

Reluctantly, Rachel laid her fingers against the man's neck, the side of her hand against his jaw.

"Doesn't seem to be any," she said after moving her fingertips carefully over the cool skin.

"We'd better phone the police, then," Matthew declared as Rachel rose and reached for the flashlight.

Rachel clasped his free hand and they started back around the barn. As they neared the small door, she asked, "Do you think I should get a blanket or something to cover him in case he is alive?"

"He's evidently not, Rachel; don't worry," he answered, pressing her fingers gently.

Rachel's heart was heavy as they walked up the lane to the house.

The kitchen window welcomed them through the darkness with its usual cheeriness. Climbing the porch steps and stepping into the cozy room, Rachel found it hard to realize there actually *was* a dead man out behind the barn.

While Matthew went into the front hall to make the necessary phone calls, she brewed a pot of coffee—then sat at the kitchen table to wait.

Whose body is that out behind the barn? she wondered.

Does he have a family? Is his wife frantic not knowing where he is? Does he have children who are wondering where Daddy is? Did he know about the love of God, the sacrifice of the Lord Jesus for him, before he faced eternity?

Wondering about the story behind that poor man made him seem more real to her. Instead of a horrible, frightening *thing* out in the overgrown weeds, the form became a man. A man unknown to her, but about whom she was growing more concerned.

A soft but distinctive sound in the distance kept increasing in volume and shrillness until it registered in Rachel's mind as sirens.

Becoming louder and louder as they approached, they finally stopped all at once.

She heard the motors of vehicles coming to a halt in the drive alongside the big house, car doors slamming, and the slight tapping of Matthew's cane as he went to the front door.

Feeling suddenly very tired, Rachel rose from her chair and went to join Matthew and the men who had just entered the foyer.

At Matthew's introduction, Chief Turner smiled at Rachel.

"We've met," he said. "This is my partner, Barton Thomas; Mark Perkins and Ed Marsh are just coming in. They're two of our Emergency Medics. Now, if you'll direct us to where the body is . . ."

"I'll go, Matthew," Rachel offered. "You really should rest your leg."

"Thanks, Rachel, but I'll walk part way."

Following her, the five men trooped down the hall, through the kitchen and back porch, and down the steps.

"Follow that lane over there," she said, pointing. "I'll catch up with you in a minute."

Turning to Matthew, she put her hand on his arm, "You look as though you're in pain. Please just go to your cottage and rest your leg. I'll be all right—I'm not as frightened as I was earlier."

"I will if you'll let me phone Aunt Caroline and ask her to stay here with you tonight," he answered.

"That'll be fine," Rachel agreed. "I'll call you after the men leave and let you know what they said. Please, Matt, your face was so pale in the indoor light."

"I'll go; now hurry, so you can show them where the fellow can be found."

"Bye, I'll phone," Rachel promised, running to the barn lane, the beam of her flashlight bobbing as she jogged.

Rachel stood by in the crisp weeds, sand burrs clinging to her pantlegs, watching while the medics examined the body and the policemen discussed, took notes and measured distances.

Then, the brown-suited, dark-haired man's body was lifted onto a stretcher by Ed Marsh and Mark Perkins, their forms becoming dark, shadowy figures among the trees. They lifted the stretcher and, carrying it, soon disappeared around the far corner of the huge barn.

"Afraid I'll have to ask you some questions, Miss," Chief Turner said. "But since it's getting late, how about if I come by in the morning, say about ten?"

"That'll be fine," Rachel answered as they left the scene together and started down the lane.

"We'll need to check the barn and land around here," the chief continued. "See what we can find that might have some bearing on this crime."

"I'll cooperate in whatever way I can," Rachel assured him.

"Will you have to question the children and young people who were here?" she asked, hoping they wouldn't have to be involved.

"We'll want to talk to the ones who discovered the body; may talk briefly with the others. Can you give me names and addresses of those who were here tonight?"

"I'm sure Tassie Wolcott can. Her little brother was one of the children who found the dead man."

"Fine," Chief Turner said. "He's the little fellow who brought in that fish trophy, isn't he?"

"Yes, his grandmother, Caroline Wolcott, works with me at the inn, so he plays around here a lot."

"He may have noticed some little thing lately that will help," the chief said. "Where do his parents live?"

"He was orphaned when quite small. Now he lives with

Mrs. Wolcott," Rachel told him. "Would you care for a cup of coffee before you leave? I have some ready."

"Thanks, Miss Hoekstra, don't mind if I do. How about you, Bart?"

"Sure—always ready for a cup of something hot after a long day," said the man trudging along at Rachel's other side.

In the kitchen, as the two uniformed men drained their second cups of coffee and emptied a small plate of donuts left from the party, Rachel began to feel uneasy, realizing she would be alone in a few minutes.

The sense of fear that had rushed over her when Aaron first told of discovering the body began to press against her again. Her throat became dry and her breath a little short.

"Chief Turner," she began, realizing she was having difficulty making her voice sound normal, "do you have any idea who the dead man is, or why he would be on my property?"

"Haven't the foggiest idea at present, Miss Hoekstra," he answered. "May have something to do with the recent truck hijacking, but such inconsequential items hardly seem reason for murder, so there's probably no connection."

"You do think it was murder, then?" Rachel asked, an eerie sensation moving up her back.

"Sorry, don't know that; I'm talking out of turn. Really shouldn't even be discussing it yet."

He pushed his chair back, scraping it along the kitchen tile. "Better be shoving off, Bart," he said, picking up his hat and notebook.

"Thanks for the welcome refreshments, Miss Hoekstra," he added as they walked through the doorway into the hall. "See you tomorrow about ten."

After they left, Rachel locked the door and returned to the kitchen to do the same there.

She had just finished rinsing the coffee cups and was preparing to wash the coffeepot when she heard a vehicle approaching along the house's side drive.

Rachel noted its familiar sound and remembered Matthew had said he would phone Aunt Caroline. Peeking around the drawn blind, Rachel recognized the truck just before the headlights and dash lights flicked off.

Unlocking the door, she hurried out to greet her friend, taking the overnight case from her as she emerged slowly from the truck.

"I seem to be getting more stiff in the knees lately," she commented before slamming the reluctant door.

"I'm glad you're here, Aunt Caroline." Rachel put her free arm around the other woman's ample shoulders for a brief hug.

"I suppose it's silly to be nervous here alone, but I can't shake the feeling after what happened tonight," she continued as they climbed the steps to the porch. "I was relieved when Matthew said he was going to call you."

"Don't blame you one bit," Aunt Caroline assured her. "I'd be on edge myself, not knowing who that man was, why he'd been around here."

"Or who killed him and where they are now." Rachel's quiet voice quavered a bit.

"Well, let's not fret about it tonight." Aunt Caroline dropped into a chair at the kitchen table.

"Wouldn't mind some coffee, child, if you have some left you can just heat up," she said with a sigh, stretching her aching legs under the table.

Rachel put the still-hot pot of coffee over a low flame and got two mugs from the cupboard. After putting them on the table with a small pitcher of cream, she bent to put her arms around Aunt Caroline, laying her rosy white cheek against the dark black one.

Tendrils of Rachel's flowing blonde hair entwined with Aunt Caroline's gray-black braids.

"I shouldn't have let Matthew phone you," Rachel scolded herself. "You seem tired. Then to have to drive over here at a time when you were probably hoping to get to bed. It makes me feel like a real baby."

Aunt Caroline chuckled. "Honey, I feel about ready for bed even during the day sometimes. I didn't mind a bit, Matthew asking me to come over. I was happy, actually; makes me feel you both consider me your close friend."

"I *do*, Aunt Caroline," Rachel assured her, going for the coffee and pouring each of them a steaming cup.

Slowly stirring in an ample portion of cream, Aunt Caroline confided, "My sister, Lonnie, wants me and the children to move up to Michigan and live with her. She and Jedediah have more than enough room, and it would be nice for Aaron—living on a big farm."

"Do you plan on going? I'd sure miss you," Rachel said.

"I'd miss you, too, child. Aaron likes it here, but would like very much to go. He and his Uncle Jed get along like father and son; that part would benefit him, too."

Rachel waited, not sure how much the older woman wanted to tell her, and she didn't want to pry.

Aunt Caroline sipped at her coffee.

"Tassie and Todd would like to get married some time in the next year, so naturally she doesn't want to leave here and have to be away from him."

"She hadn't mentioned that to me," Rachel said, feeling a bit slighted.

"She just told me last weekend; she planned to tell you soon, and hoped you wouldn't think she was too young."

"I guess age often has little to do with maturity," Rachel stated, adding with a light laugh, "Sometimes lately, with the responsibility here, I feel at least forty."

"Know what you mean." Aunt Caroline passed her cup for a refill. "Todd is twenty-two, a fine young man. He loves the Lord, and comes from a Christian family. Has a decent position in a nearby school system, so I really have no reservations about the marriage."

"If you want to move to your sister's home, Tassie could live here with me. I'd welcome her company. That way, she could keep the good job she has and be near Todd.

"I doubt I'll have tourist guests at the inn now until spring, so I would just need to cook for the two of us."

"Bless you for the offer, Rachel; I hadn't even thought of that possibility. I may speak to her about it."

Aunt Caroline set her mug aside and heaved herself up from the chair, her palms pressed hard against the tabletop. "If you'll excuse me now, I think I'll head for bed."

As she left the kitchen, the phone rang; Rachel hurried to answer it.

"I thought I saw a glint of light through the trees and realized you must still be up. Aunt Caroline get there okay?"

"Yes, Matthew, thanks. She's very tired—just went to her room," Rachel answered.

"If you two need anything, be sure to call me; anytime, you understand?"

"Thank you, Matthew. It's good to know you're close by."

There was silence for several moments; then he spoke again, his voice especially gentle.

"Rachel, I . . ."

"Yes?

"Matthew?" she said when there was no reply.

"Good night, Rachel," came his quiet response. "Sleep well."

She heard the soft click of his receiver and, humming as she went back to the kitchen, began washing the coffeepot, an enchanted smile on her lips.

Chapter Thirteen

Chief Turner arrived on time the next morning. Rachel went with him to the barn where he probed the area inside, questioning her as they went.

Then, back outside in the brisk, cool air and sunshine of a fine autumn day, they trampled around the barn to the spot where last night's gruesome discovery had lain.

Officer Thomas and several other uniformed young men were methodically searching through the underbrush behind the large barn.

"When you finish here, fan out and check along the edge of the bluff!" Chief Turner shouted to them. "Then cover the side of the hill down to the river."

He turned to Rachel. "Notice how the weeds seem to have been trampled in a straight line from where the body was toward the edge of the bluff? Almost as though someone's been along that route often enough to form a path."

"No, I hadn't," she answered, walking in that direction to take a look.

He's right, she said to herself. *I hardly think Aaron could have done that.*

Chief Turner walked up beside her, saying to Officer Thomas, who had joined him with an object in his hand, "Looks as though something was dragged through that tall, dry grass."

Rachel shivered slightly, remembering the sprawled body in the brown suit.

"Why would someone kill that man, then drag him up here?" she asked, perplexed.

"Don't know as that happened. He was probably shot right

here. That path was made by something larger than a person."

"Whatta you make of this?" Officer Thomas asked, extending his gloved hand, which held a weather damaged book titled *Taxidermy Made Easy*.

"Where'd you find that?"

"At the edge of the trampled path area over there."

Chief Turner turned the book over, pursing his lips, then slipped it into a plastic bag he took from his pocket.

"I'm going back to the office soon," he said. "You fellows find anything, bring it in. If you come across something that warrants my coming back out here, give me a call."

"Right," Officer Thomas acknowledged, turning to join the others. His boots crunched through the tall, dry grass toward the end of the barn. Chief Turner joined Rachel.

"No I.D. on him, Miss Hoekstra; his prints will be checked in Indianapolis. We don't have a computer hook-up here, so everything takes longer than in a city."

They crunched along the lane to the back of the inn, sunshine bright upon them, unobstructed by the now leafless trees towering above.

As they neared the house, she said, "I started a pot of coffee when you arrived. May I give you some?"

"I'm in a bit of a hurry, but can't usually refuse an offer like that," he grinned. "Seem to smell something spicy from the direction of the kitchen, too."

"Aunt Caroline must be baking something," Rachel said, laughing lightly. "That dear lady always seems to be busy."

Chief Turner's guess was a good one; the warmth of the kitchen was permeated with the aroma of apples mingled with nutmeg and cinnamon, brown sugar and raisins.

"Ummm," he said appreciatively, removing his hat.

"Morning, ma'am," he said to Aunt Caroline, who was turning from the oven, her mitt-covered hands cradling a bubbling pan of syrupy apple dumplings.

"Suppose you'd like to sample these?" she said, a teasing smile crinkling her face.

"If they're like the ones I remember from the time you did some baking for my mother, I sure wouldn't mind." He stepped over to help her.

While Rachel poured coffee for the three of them, she pondered the recent unusual events and discoveries near the old barn. Had it not been as deserted as everyone supposed? And what about the stuffed fish and the bag containing the plaster of Paris Aaron had found? Then the dead man and the book on taxidermy. Was there a connection somewhere?

"Chief Turner," she began, pouring cream over the apple-filled pastries Aunt Caroline had just dished up, "do you suppose the taxidermy book has some bearing on the fact that the hijacked truck found near here was carrying items prepared by taxidermists?"

"Same question's been running around in my head," he answered. "Seems plausible, but so far I can't connect it with any reason for murder." He carefully tasted the thick hot syrup and flaky pastry on his spoon.

"You believe that man was murdered for sure?" Aunt Caroline asked.

"Quite sure; he was shot in the back . . . twice."

"Tsk, Tsk," Aunt Caroline clucked her tongue. "Who'd ever have expected something like that in a quiet little area like Wedgewood; especially way out here by Mulberry Inn. I've never seen the like!"

"Afraid violence is no respecter of places, Mrs. Wolcott," he said. "You sure do know how to bake tasty desserts. My wife's a fine cook, but she doesn't bake a lot. It's been a long time since I've had apples fixed this way."

When he'd finished eating and drained his cup, he asked if he could stop by Caroline's home that afternoon to talk to Aaron, and she agreed.

The following days brought much conjecturing and little additional evidence of strangers on the inn property, except for the discovery of a handgun in the weeds and a metal can of glue, near the river's edge, behind the barn.

"The weapon's been wiped clean of fingerprints," Chief Turner told Rachel. "And the numbers were filed off, but it seems to be the one used on Charles Palmer."

"Oh, you've traced his identity," Rachel said.

"Only his name, no current address. Had him on a drug bust a couple of years ago in Indianapolis, but it didn't stick."

Thinking about their conversation later, Rachel wondered if the glue can was what she saw reflecting the sunlight one day recently, instead of Aaron's homemade metal submarine, as she'd thought.

"Some of the things found around here seem to belong in a craft class," she mused. "Glue and plaster of Paris—sure is strange.

The first week of November brought cold winds and gray skies with only a day of sunshine.

With straw Matthew had gotten from the man who bought his dad's farm, Rachel covered the perennial beds and the strawberry and asparagus patches.

"It's worth the work," Aunt Caroline told her. "And you can use the straw to mulch your vegetable garden next summer if you plant one."

Summer seemed far away to Rachel; the coming winter stretched ahead of her. She was beginning to feel the cold loneliness she had expected to come eventually.

Matthew was leaving for another month at the Rehab Center.

"Then I'm to stay with my folks until mid-December, at least," he said as he was saying goodbye at her door after a special meal together.

"A friend has offered me a job in the city near my folks, and I've promised to at least consider.

"The income would be very good, Rachel, with a fine chance for advancement." His voice held an edge of excitement.

"I thought you said one day you hoped to work with young people, teaching or maybe coaching," Rachel said quietly, trying to keep the faint pleading from her voice.

"I did, I *do*. But there's nothing open around here right now, Rachel. I've checked into it, hoping to stay in this area, to be where I can see you . . . spend time with you."

She nodded, her head lowered, tears beginning to well up in her eyes. She blinked them back just as she felt his finger under her chin, lifting gently, forcing her to look at him.

"Rachel, my heart is filled with things I want to say to you; I want to so very much."

Matthew's voice sounded ragged, and suddenly broke; he could say no more.

Instead, he put his cane-free arm around her shoulders, pulling her against him for a moment.

Rachel felt his chest heave against her cheek as he sighed deeply.

"Whatever happens regarding the job, I plan to be back here for Christmas." He tried to make his voice sound light.

"I already know where I'll put my little Christmas tree in the cottage."

Stepping away from her, he clasped her hand, saying, "Walk as far as the rail fence just beyond the root-cellar mound with me."

There, with the last rays of sun slanting low on the horizon in a gold-tinged sky, the cold breeze chilling their faces, he bent and kissed her forehead in farewell.

Rachel watched him go beneath the bare-limbed trees, his feet scuffling through drifts of dry leaves.

She stood there until he disappeared among the evergreen bushes; then she turned to retrace her way to the inn, still feeling the warm, light touch of his lips.

Chapter Fourteen

The following week was a lonely one for Rachel. She missed Matthew more than she'd ever missed anyone, and was even busier than usual.

Just knowing Matthew wasn't in the carriage house made her heart feel hollow—empty somehow.

Instinctively, before retiring at night, she glanced in that direction, anticipating the time when he would be back. The time would come when lights would be glowing from his windows again.

One night, out of habit, she glanced casually through her upstairs window while brushing her hair—and paused, startled, her brush in midair.

Was her imagination playing tricks, or was that a light she had seen in the distance?

"You're pretending to see what you wish was there," she chided herself, brushing her hair back over her shoulders.

"Besides, that flick of light was nowhere near Matthew's cottage."

She put the brush on the dressing table and started to remove her robe, still thinking about the light.

It was over by the barn . . . The barn! her thoughts exploded, and she hurried back to the window.

One hand on the windowsill, she parted the lacy curtains, peering through the darkness, seeing nothing unusual.

Kneeling on the braided rug, she watched awhile, but only bare black branches moved in the wind. The dark sky was pricked in spots by stars; the others were hidden behind clouds.

"Lord," she prayed, "I feel very much on edge alone here after what's been happening. The doors are locked and I suppose I'm perfectly safe; I'm not taking foolish chances. Please help me to know you are with me; help me to sleep well."

Rachel paused, sighing, "And, Lord, help Matthew strengthen his body. Give him wisdom concerning your will in the job offer. Show him definitely what he's to do with his life at this particular time.

"If he could move permanently near Wedgewood and serve you in some way, please show him that. Amen."

Rachel rose, closed the curtains and padded across to her bed, feeling quieted and a little uneasy at the same time.

The mid-November days continued dull and gray with occasional light snow flurries.

Aaron came on Saturdays to help Rachel rake leaves from the large front lawn, piling them in ancient fenced-in compost bins by the garden area opposite the storm-cellar mound.

Afterward, they made a bonfire of a pile of leaves they'd reserved for it and roasted hot dogs and marshmallows.

"These long-handled forks work great," Aaron said, as juices dripping from the hot dog spattered and crackled in the flames.

"I think they're very old," Rachel said. "I found them in the pantry in a big drawer full of cutlery. I found a pocket knife, too—saved it for you."

"Oh, boy!" Aaron exclaimed, reaching for one of the oblong sesame-topped buns warming on a piece of foil near the fire.

"Did you ever hear anything from the police about the fish you found?" Rachel asked, spooning relish on her hot sandwich.

"Naw, not yet." Aaron reached for the bottle of ketchup nestled against a stone. "Suppose they forgot all about it by now."

Considering recent events, Rachel wasn't so sure, but she mentioned none of this to him. Instead, she took a bite of her tasty sandwich, sniffing the good smell of burning leaves.

Tassie and Aunt Caroline came early in the evening for the simple supper Rachel had ready following her invitation. They brought with them a pie made from cherries canned the previous spring.

"Sure can tell what you two've been doing," Tassie said, placing the pie on the counter and removing her coat. "I can smell the smoke on you."

"It was fun," Aaron said. "We had a bonfire. You should have been here, Tassie."

"Todd and I were visiting with his folks," she answered her nephew, but glanced at Rachel.

"They and Mama have all given their permission and blessing for us to be married," she smiled at Rachel.

"Oh, Tassie, I'm so happy for you!" Rachel exclaimed, putting down the soup ladle to hug her friend.

"I can't wait to hear about your plans for the wedding."

"I'm hoping you'll help me make them," Tassie said.

"Oh, I'd love to, Tassie; it would be an honor."

Tassie's smile widened, her face glowing. "And I want *you* to be my maid-of-honor."

"I'll be delighted to," Rachel declared, giving her another quick hug.

"I wish you two would sit down," Aaron interjected, unimpressed by their excitement. "I'm hungry."

"As usual," his aunt said fondly, tousling his hair.

Later, while Rachel was cutting the pie, Aunt Caroline said, "We'd like very much for you to join us in our home for Thanksgiving dinner, Rachel.

"Tassie said you didn't plan to be with your family, and you seem like part of ours. Will you come?"

"Sure I will. May I bring desserts?" Rachel offered.

"Well, you needn't do that, child," Aunt Caroline chuckled. "Just bring yourself."

"Why don't you have her make some of that great chocolate fudge she brought one time for Tassie's birthday?" Aaron suggested eagerly.

"All right, if she wants to," his mother replied. "I thought he might have some ideas," she added laughingly, looking at Rachel.

"Fudge it is, then," Rachel declared. "What time should I come?"

"Come as early as you like, honey," Aunt Caroline said. "We'll plan on having dinner ready at noon, so we can take a meal to Mrs. Ching, who's not feeling well, and a couple of other folks who'll be alone but don't want to go out. We'll plan our own dinner for about 1:30."

"In that case, I'll make some extra batches of candy and come early enough to help with preparations," Rachel volunteered. "I'll bake some cookies, too, to add to the boxes—and small dried flower arrangements to brighten their tables."

The following week, Rachel delved into the pantry's ample supply of dishes, selecting three squat pottery bowls of soft yellow, banded in brown and gold.

She filled them with some of the colorful leaves, dried seed pods, flowers and tall golden grasses she'd gathered earlier. When they were arranged to her satisfaction, she put each, centered on a crocheted doily from the attic, in a shallow scrubbed grape basket.

Pleased with the results, Rachel lined the baskets up on one end of the table, ready to receive the fudge and cookies she would make in a few days.

On Wednesday, Rachel received a lovely card from Matthew in the mail. A brilliant red cardinal was pictured on the front. Inside, he'd written:

As Thanksgiving approaches,
I've been thinking about the things
for which I'm most thankful.
Rachel, you are very special to me.
I thank Jesus for bringing you into my life.
Matthew

Thanksgiving Day began with bright sunshine on one horizon, and gray, slow-moving clouds approaching from the northwest on the other.

Oh, dear, Rachel thought, when at midmorning she noticed the clouds had moved closer. *I wonder if the weather will turn bad before we can get the dinners delivered.*

She was glad Tassie would be by for her in a few minutes so she could help her and Aunt Caroline.

The young women hurriedly slipped the pretty baskets into an immense cardboard box covered with a plastic sheet that was already in the truck bed.

Anchoring the plastic with several rocks, Tassie said, "This is ready for the dinners. Mama keeps little insulated hampers on hand for these occasions. They get the food there still nice and hot."

"You folks think of everything," Rachel declared. "I don't think I've ever met a family as generous and willing to help as yours."

"Thanks, Rachel," Tassie said quietly. "Mama's always taught us, and showed us, that this was a way we could express Jesus' love to others.

"And a way of working out the scripture verse that says what we do for others in need, we do for Him."

Tassie's old home was beginning to show its age and lack of finances for upkeep. Bright sunshine revealed clapboards with peeling paint and curled-up edges on some roof shingles.

But the lawn was neatly raked, and mum plants, tightly hanging on to their last yellow and gold blooms, were clustered around the front steps.

Inside, the rooms of outdated but neat furniture were filled with the aroma of roasting chickens, herb dressing, and honeyed sweet potatoes.

"Looks like you're cooking for all of Wedgewood," Rachel laughed, giving Aunt Caroline a hug.

Counters were crowded with pies and pans of dinner rolls, containers of cranberry sauce, assorted pickles, and jellies.

Aunt Caroline opened the oven door, which sent out more of the marvelous aroma of baked chicken.

"Take those extra pot holders and help me with these, will you, girls?" She quickly wrapped several thicknesses of foil over the meat and its pan.

"Put each in one of these big boxes," she instructed, snuggling hers in beside casseroles of potatoes and mixed vegetables.

"Then put a thick pad of newspaper over these hot things," she went on, tucking in a pan of rolls.

"The pie and other things can go on top."

Next, she turned to Aaron. "Get your hat and coat on; help us get these under cover in the truck as quickly as possible.

"You may go with the girls to deliver them to Mrs. Ching, the Martins and old Mr. Taylor.

"And Aaron," she added, as he turned to run from the room, "remember the most important thing: give them a hug when you say goodbye."

Rachel, too, found herself giving them each a hug as they left the small, humble homes. Given not because of Aunt Caroline's suggestion, but with sincere warmth in response to the love shining in the eyes and smiles of the gentle people they visited.

By the time the old truck returned with the young people, the sun had disappeared behind the gray cloud mass moving slowly in from the horizon.

"Brrr, that wind's getting colder," Aaron announced, bounding down from the truck and racing for the front door.

In the small dining room, the table, prepared ahead of time, was festive with blue-willow dishes and a centerpiece of polished fresh fruit.

When the browned-to-perfection chicken, the bowls of dressing, gravy and vegetables had been carried from the warm oven, Aunt Caroline asked God's blessing on the food and the ones gathered around the table.

After her "amen," Tassie slipped out to the kitchen, returning with a napkin-covered basket of piping hot rolls. She placed them on the table while her mother opened a well-worn Bible and began to read from Psalm 100:

Make a joyful noise unto the Lord, all ye lands.
Serve the Lord with gladness: come before his presence
    with singing.
Know ye that the Lord he is God:
It is he that hath made us, and not we ourselves;
We are his people, and the sheep of his pasture.
Enter into his gates with thanksgiving, and into his courts
    with praise:
Be thankful unto him and bless his name.
For the Lord is good; his mercy is everlasting,
And his truth endureth to all generations.

The mood around the table was lively with banter and chatter, laughter and good-natured teasing while they ate.

"When you're done with your pie, Rachel," Aaron said from across the table, forking in the last morsel of his pumpkin-pecan dessert, "how 'bout coming up to my bedroom and seeing my rock collection and my arrowheads."

"Okay with me," she answered with a questioning glance at Aunt Caroline.

"You two go ahead when you're finished," Tassie said. "I'll clear the table and start the dishes."

"I'll dry them when I come back down," Rachel said with a smile.

As she finished her pie and coffee, Aunt Caroline suggested, "Speaking of bedrooms, why don't you spend the night with us, Rachel?"

"I can loan you pajamas and whatever else you need," Tassie offered. "Do stay."

"All right," Rachel agreed. "I'd like that."

Upstairs in Aaron's room, Rachel gave him all her attention, scrutinizing the assortment of unusual rocks and stones displayed on his dresser, then exclaiming over the small box of arrowheads, while she sat on the edge of his bed.

"Where did you find these?" she asked.

"Oh, around," he answered. "I find the unusual rocks in lots of different places. The arrowheads come to the top of the ground when the farmers plow for spring planting."

"They do? I didn't know that."

"Yeah, and I guess the weather does it sometimes, too, 'cause I've found some laying around other places."

Aaron turned from putting the box back in a dresser drawer.

"Hey, look, it's snowing real hard. Isn't it pretty?"

Rachel joined him at the window and they marveled at how quickly the small flakes joined each other to form a thin white cover on the slanted roof of the back porch below them.

"Crawled out there once when I was little," Aaron confessed. "Almost slid off 'cause it's so steep. Mama sure was scared." Then he added, a bit sheepishly, "I was pretty scared, too."

Later in the evening, after Aaron had brought his houseguest, Kiepuras' dog, Holly, up from the basement for her last run of the day, he pleaded, "Grandmama, couldn't I please let her sleep in my room tonight? She's been awful good the times she's been up there. She doesn't get into anything, honest."

"Oh, all right, honey. I guess there's no reason why she shouldn't," his grandmother answered, saying softly to Rachel,

"The way those two get along, you'd think Holly was a real person-friend to him. She seems to understand everything he says; minds him real well, too, considering she belongs to someone else."

Tassie and Rachel were slicing leftover chicken and bread and setting out pickles and other items for sandwiches when he came back to the kitchen, Holly close behind him.

"Smells sort of funny down there," he said, wrinkling his nose.

"Funny, how?" his aunt asked.

"I dunno, just funny. Sorta like the kitchen that day the oven didn't light right away when we were baking cookies. But only a little bit."

"You mean gas," Tassie said, putting down the mayonnaise jar and butter dish. "I'd better check after supper. The pilot light may have gone out on our old clothes dryer; it did once before. I'll have to relight it."

When they pushed back their chairs following a pleasant meal, Aunt Caroline said, "It's almost eight o'clock. If you young people will excuse me, I think I'll go to my room and read a while before bed."

"You *do* look tired, Grandmama," Aaron said. "Me and Holly will go on upstairs now. We'll be real quiet."

"Thanks, honey," she said, hugging him.

"It'll be good to get into a robe and slippers tonight." She shuffled as she went to her room down the hall next to the living room.

"Mama was up early today getting things ready for the extra dinners," Tassie explained. "I tried to get her to sleep a bit later, and said I'd get the chickens and vegetables ready, but she had decided to make extra pies in case someone stopped by today."

"Know what she did with them?" Tassie laughed lightly, shaking her head. "Carried them to the Watsons while we were delivering the dinners."

"The Watsons? Where do they live?" Rachel asked.

"In an old mobile home about a block from here," Tassie explained. "Mama's called on them, welcoming them to the neighborhood and inviting them to church, but she said they haven't seemed very friendly.

"She keeps trying, though," Tassie added, wiping the table and rinsing the sponge she was using.

When the few dishes had been washed, Tassie suggested, "Aaron said the snow had stopped when he came in with Holly before supper. Want to take a walk? I love to be out in the snow at night."

"Sounds like fun," Rachel said. "I'm glad I brought my boots and hooded jacket today."

The sharp, clear air made their noses tingle when they first stepped outside. The clouds had moved on and the sky was sprinkled with stars. A half moon had risen, causing the thin snow cover to sparkle.

"It snowed just enough to make everything beautiful," Rachel commented. "I'm so glad you suggested coming out. I don't remember ever being out on a winter night just to stroll."

"Mama used to take us," Tassie said. "But I knew she'd be too weary to join us tonight. She may not want to at all this year, because her legs bother her a lot."

When they were returning from their walk around the neighborhood, camouflaged in its fluffy white dress, and were in view of the Wolcott house, Tassie said, "Aaron's light is out, Mama's too; they must both be asleep.

"If you're in the mood, I'll make hot chocolate and show you pictures of Todd when he was a little boy, and the boys he coaches now."

She was just finishing her sentence when Rachel, staring in disbelief, saw what looked like a small ball of fire erupt from a basement window.

Inside the house, plumes of fire shot through a heat register into the living room, licking hungrily at the draperies, dancing crazily in the window.

Rachel's voice seemed stuck in her throat. She clutched frantically at Tassie's sleeve, pointing in the direction of Tassie's home.

Then Rachel's voice jerked free, screaming, "Tassie! Your house! It's burning! It's on fire!"

Chapter Fifteen

"Mama! Aaron!" Tassie's screams pierced through the serenity of the white landscape.

Propelled by terror, the girls sprinted down the road. Swift seconds seemed long minutes as they raced slipping and sliding up the long drive.

Living room windows were awash in flames when they reached the house.

"Back door, back door!" Tassie yelled breathlessly, heading along the side of the building.

Up the steps of the back porch they stumbled in their haste, Rachel grabbing Tassie's coat as she slipped on the covering of snow.

Tassie wrenched free, her hand already in her coat pocket gripping the keys, instinctively selecting the correct one.

Panting heavily, she groped in the darkness for the keyhole, beginning to sob with fear and frustration.

Tearing off her gloves, Rachel felt for the keyhole and, grabbing Tassie's shaking hand, guided the key, helping Tassie turn it.

Flinging open the door, Tassie began to scream, "Mama, where are you! Mama! Aaron!" Sobs rising in her throat choked out her cries.

"Tassie! Hush!" Rachel yelled, grabbing her friend, stopping her headlong flight across the room. "We've got to be calm! Now listen!" Talking fast, Rachel spoke loudly, "Get a couple of towels and wet them to hold over your faces if necessary; get your mom from her room and take her outside!

"Quickly!" Rachel shoved Tassie toward the sink.

"I'll go upstairs for Aaron."

Rachel turned back and snapped on the kitchen light, thankful the electricity was still on.

Tassie jerked open a drawer, grabbed towels and turned the faucet on full force.

Rachel pulled the dish towels from the rack on the wall and dropped them into the water swirling in the sink.

"Show us what to do, God," she prayed urgently, plunging the towels up and down in the water.

Then, both girls raced toward the front of the house, yelling, "Fire! Fire!" Tassie slammed open her mother's door, while Rachel passed her, making a mad dash toward the flaming front of the house to head upstairs.

"Help me, Lord Jesus," she cried aloud, "guide me."

The living room had become an inferno, its heat blasting out at Rachel as she turned just short of it to sprint up the staircase.

She heard windows bursting and shattering as she neared the second floor.

Above her, at the top of the stairs, was darkness. *Will I even be able to find Aaron?* she frantically wondered. *I hope Tassie can get to a neighbor's to phone the fire department.*

By the time she reached the upstairs hall, Aaron was standing at the far end dressed in his pajamas, illuminated by a shaft of light from his room.

"Fire, Aaron!" Rachel yelled, racing toward him. "Get your coat!"

But he was trying to pick up Holly and wasn't concerned about anything else.

Rachel grabbed his coat from a chair just as the light went out.

Electricity's gone, she realized. "Aaron," she commanded, "go straight to the window! Quickly!"

"What's happening?" he asked. "Me and Holly was just getting to sleep."

Rachel groped her way across the room to the window, glad she'd been there earlier so its layout was a bit familiar.

In the darkness, she joined him at the window, awkwardly forcing his arms one by one into the sleeves of his coat, while he tried to hang on to a squirming, whining Holly.

"Is there *really* a fire, Rachel?" he gasped.

Then as the enormity of it registered, he cried, "Grandmama! Where's Grandmama?" and turned to run from the room.

Rachel grabbed him, still with his arms entwined around Holly, and put him firmly against the wall next to the window. She could smell the smoke beginning to send its deadly tendrils into the room.

"Grandmama's okay, Aaron. Tassie took her outside," Rachel stated firmly, praying it was so. "Now you stay right here for a minute," she added emphatically.

Groping her way back to his doorway, she found the end of the hall, lit by the flames that were beginning to devour the stairway.

Turning, she shouted, "Are there other stairs beside the ones from near the front door, Aaron?"

"No," he answered, his voice beginning to reveal his fear. "Why don't we get out of here, Rachel?" his voice quavered.

"We will, Aaron, right away. Where are your shoes or boots?"

"Shoes are under the chair," he answered, his voice rising; "boots in the closet. But I don't need them! Please, let's go!"

Smoke was beginning to drift more heavily into the room, bringing heat with it. Rachel slammed the door, groping for Aaron's shoes under the chair.

Finding them, she picked up the wet towels in her other hand and returned quickly to the window.

"Put Holly down!" she commanded. "Take her collar with one hand. Hold this towel against your face if the smoke gets heavier."

"Okay," he answered meekly, complying.

"Hush, Holly," she said to the whining dog as she slipped Aaron's bare feet into his shoes. She unlocked the window and tried to open it. It wouldn't budge.

Again and again she tried to force the sash upward.

Moisture must have frozen the window shut, one part of her mind told her logically; while her frenzied thoughts tried to find a way of smashing the window without either of them getting cut.

"Turn your back—and stay that way!" she ordered, going for the chair. "I'll have to break the window."

Averting her face as much as possible, she swung the chair hard.

The glass broke with a loud crash, falling to the floor and the roof outside through the smashed screen.

"Don't look yet, Aaron!" she said, coughing, hurrying through the dark smoke-filled room to the dresser.

Groping for his largest rock, she felt the nearby door.

It was searing hot, the varnish melting and peeling.

With a cry she drew back, hurried to the window and broke out the remaining glass with the rock. Choking and coughing, Rachel found her way to Aaron's bed. Pulling off the blankets and pillow, she spread a blanket over the glass shards under the window, put the pillow across the windowsill, and spread the other blanket outside.

"C'mon, Aaron! Hurry!" she shouted, while trying to sound calm. She grabbed his arm, noticing how hot the floor was getting.

"We're going out the window."

"It's steep and slippery out there; we'll slide right off!" he screamed, straining away from her grasp. "Let's go down the stairs!"

"We can't!" Rachel said sternly, pulling him back. "They're burning."

Coughing, Aaron shoved the towel back against his face.

"I'll help you out first, then Holly." Rachel's voice left no room for argument. "Now! Come on!"

Holly clung tightly against Aaron's legs as he stepped on the blanket, crunching the glass underneath.

Following Rachel's instructions, and with her help, Aaron boosted himself onto the pillow, twisted his body and put his legs over the windowsill, dangling them above the slanted roof below.

"I'll hold your hands while you get your feet on the roof, Aaron," she encouraged him.

"Tell me as soon as you touch it."

"Now!" he yelled a moment later, sliding out the window. "Hear the sirens? Firemen must be coming!"

"Thank you, Lord," Rachel breathed.

"Aaron, move away from the window a bit, then sit on the roof with your back against the house!" she shouted, leaning out the window, still firmly gripping one of his hands.

When he was situated as safely as possible, she said, "I'll try to lift Holly out there. Reach over and grab her collar and pull her against you."

The struggling, frightened little dog proved almost more than Rachel could handle. Finally, resting her weight on the pillowed ledge, she lowered Holly to where Aaron could reach her collar.

Slipping on the snowy roof, her legs flailing, Holly was urged over against Aaron, who spoke comfortingly to her, holding her tight against his side.

Rachel could see small tongues of flame licking under the closed bedroom door and knew she had to follow Aaron.

But, what'll we do when I get out there? The thought of jumping filled Rachel with dread, yet she knew she had to try to protect Aaron and herself from the flames that were fast approaching.

Downstairs, on the front lawn, neighbors were restraining a frantic Tassie who, after bringing her mother out and sending someone to call the fire department, had run back into the house intending to dash up the fire-engulfed stairway.

"My nephew, Aaron, is up there!" her voice shrilled, trying to pull away from the man who held her arms.

"Rachel's there, too! Please! Someone help them! Please! Please!" Tassie collapsed, sobbing, into the neighbor's arms, while she looked beseechingly at the small crowd that was gathering. The twirling lights on the fire trucks cast a reddish glow on the snow.

Long, heavy hoses were snaked out and fastened to a nearby hydrant: water spurted and hissed in towering fountains as it sprayed the now flaming roof.

Tassie tore loose from her comforting but helpless neighbor and headed for the back of the house with him and several bystanders running after her.

"Thank you , Lord . . ." she prayed as she ran, slipping and sliding on the loose, snow-covered gravel of the drive.

"Thank you for reminding me of Aaron's window. Please make Rachel think of it. Please don't let them die in those flames."

Tearing around the back corner of the kitchen, she looked up.

"Oh, no!" she groaned.

Aaron's window framed the dancing, devouring flames that were fast filling his room.

Tassie's eyes strained, searching; but there was no one in the window. She could see no figures in the room.

Neighbor men had caught up to her now, about to restrain her again, feeling helpless against the enveloping flames, the thick smoke.

Swirling out of the window directly above them now, the smoke obscured for a moment the flames in the room.

"Aaron!" Tassie shrieked. "Aaron! Rachel!"

"Up here!" a voice answered over the roaring of the fire and commotion on the ground.

"We're up here on the porch roof," Rachel called, stopping abruptly, coughing hard.

"Up here, Tassie—we're up here," Aaron called. "Help us—don't let the fire get us!"

"Hold on! Stay where you are!" a man's voice called to them from beside Tassie; his reassuring hand reached out to grip her arm.

"They've gone for a ladder!"

"We can't wait!" Rachel shrilled as flames reached out the window, licking along the wall toward them.

To Aaron she shouted, "Don't worry! Take my hand. We'll slide down to the edge of the roof."

"Okay!" he shouted back, trying to be brave for her sake, feeling almost a man and wanting to help her.

"I've got a good hold on Holly, too, but she's scared!" he added, shouting above the flames and the motors of vehicles arriving.

"I'm scared, too," Rachel admitted, "but we'll make it. Hang tightly to my hand now . . . let's start scooting."

Rachel's slacks were already soaked from the snow; her seat felt frozen. She could imagine the intense cold the little boy must be experiencing, bare-legged and in pajamas.

Her hands felt numb by the time they had scooted carefully, fearfully, to the edge of the roof.

She reached forward, past her bent leg and boot, to find the cold metal of the gutter. Her back was hot from the heat of the flames pouring out the window, renewing itself in the asphalt roof shingles.

Rachel turned her head and saw small, menacing flames advancing toward them, growing as they came.

When she turned back, she was blinded by the beam of a flashlight that had searched them out where they were partially silhouetted by the black smoke and against the red-gold light of the fire.

"Drop the boy and dog!" someone shouted. "We'll catch them!"

"Help me get Holly over the edge, Aaron," Rachel said firmly, afraid he wouldn't cooperate.

Fear and understanding in his eyes, he tugged Holly over to where Rachel could wrap her arm around the dog's chest.

Rachel stretched herself full length on the roof, gripped the icy gutter, and loosened her hold on Holly.

She heard cheers as the little dog landed squarely in someone's arms.

"Is she all right?" Aaron asked, his face a strange distortion in the illumination surrounding them. He broke into a fit of coughing.

"She's fine," Rachel assured him, stretching her hand out, gripping his leg, pulling gently but insistently.

"You're next, Aaron—hurry! I'll help you. I'll hold you while you turn on your tummy and slide your legs over the edge of the roof."

"But I'll fall," Aaron said, even as he did as he was told.

"No, you won't! I'll hold your wrists while you grab the gutter. Now, start sliding down."

"Here he comes!" she shouted over the roof's edge. "A little boy—get ready to catch him!"

"We're ready!" two male voices shouted in unison.

"Please, Lord," Rachel breathed, "help us do this right; don't let him get hurt."

"Let me go now, Rachel," Aaron urged in her ear; she released her numbed fingers and felt him slip from her grasp.

"Got him!" voices shouted.

"You're next, young lady!"

Gingerly Rachel began to slide her chilled, soaked body sideways over the wet snow, maneuvering so she would be sure to go over the edge feet first.

I'm positive I won't be able to grip the gutter, she realized with resignation, unable now to even bend her fingers.

I won't make it without getting hurt; I'll fall right over the edge; no one will be able to help me. I'll fall right on someone, maybe kill them. In a brief moment, Rachel's thoughts had turned fatalistic—she felt like giving up. Then, she heard Aaron's voice.

"C'mon, Rachel! Hurry! It's easy."

"Get out of the way!" she yelled. "I won't be able to hold on."

The toe of her boot caught in the gutter, she tried to grip the hot, wet roof with her elbows, then heard a shout.

"Ladder's coming—hold on! They'll carry you down!"

Intense heat from the fire and great relief enveloped her in seemingly equal amounts. Rachel dropped her head against her arm and let the tears flow for the few moments until the ladder banged against the gutter and strong arms helped her to the ground.

An hour or so later, after being bundled into blankets at a neighbor's home, they were given hot soup and comforting words. Then, Rachel and Aunt Caroline's family were driven to Mulberry Inn, where they crawled into familiar beds and fell into the deep sleep of the exhausted.

Chapter Sixteen

Following a morning of shocked disbelief over what had happened, Rachel sat at her kitchen table with Aunt Caroline, Tassie and Aaron eating a very late breakfast.

"All we have is what we're wearing," Tassie lamented for about the sixth time.

"We still got the truck," Aaron piped up encouragingly. "Good thing you parked it out by the garage and not near the house."

"Bless you for looking on the bright side," his grandmother said, her face drawn from concern and lack of sleep.

"We should be spending more time thanking God for sparing our lives and less time moaning about what we've lost." She reached across the corner of the table to pat her grandson's hand.

"You're right, Mama," Tassie responded quietly, "but we really did lose almost everything we own."

"I know," her mother answered, a small smile softening her face. "but they are only things. Necessary things can be replaced eventually; the others don't really matter."

The shrill ring of the doorbell shattered the dull silence that had begun to hover over the little group in the kitchen.

When Rachel went to answer it, the others could hear down the long hallway the low tones of a man's voice.

When Rachel returned, she handed a thick envelope to Aunt Caroline.

"It was Mr. Watson. He said he lives in a mobile home not far from your house," Rachel told her.

Aunt Caroline nodded, indicating she knew to whom Rachel was referring, and turned the envelope over before looking questioningly at Rachel.

"He and his wife visited everyone in your neighborhood this morning," Rachel continued. "Everyone included their sympathy with what they contributed to the envelope."

"Open it, Grandmama!" Aaron said. "Sure is thick—wonder what's in it!"

Tears rolled down her full dark cheeks. "I thought those folks were a mite unfriendly; they were just shy, I guess. Or maybe they were embarrassed 'cause they didn't want to attend church when I invited them."

"The envelope, Grandmama," Aaron repeated. "Open it."

Smiling, she handed it to her impatient grandson. "You may open it," she said.

Poking a finger under an unsealed corner of the flap, he ripped the envelope open.

"Oh, boy!" he bellowed, "look, Grandmama, look!"

Aaron turned the envelope upside down, shaking it. Out tumbled currency of various denominations—fives, tens, twenties.

"Looks like the Lord's provided our train fare," Aunt Caroline informed Rachel. "Aaron and I will be here only a few more days, I think."

"Where we goin', Grandmama?" Aaron asked, sorting the bills into little piles.

"Going to live with your Uncle Jed and Aunt Lonnie, if they still want us," she answered. "I plan to phone them this afternoon to tell them what happened to our home."

"Oh, boy!" Aaron exclaimed.

"Aunt Caroline, you know you're welcome to stay here indefinitely. I have plenty of room, and we all get along so well."

"I know, honey . . . thank you. Tassie will probably want to stay, but I think it's best that Aaron and I make this move now. You know I've been considering it; last night just makes the time more definite."

Around noon, Rev. Harbrous arrived with another envelope of currency, one with an ample gift certificate from a Wedgewood clothing store, and assurances of the prayers of the Wolcotts' friends at the church. He also brought their many and varied offers of assistance.

By that evening Aunt Caroline had finalized plans for her move to Michigan.

The following day, Saturday, after insistent pleading by Aaron, Tassie agreed to drive by their burned home on the way back from Wedgewood where she was to oversee getting him some new clothes.

"Good thing I left some jeans and a shirt here at your house, Rachel," he grinned, "or I'd be going into town in my pajamas."

Aunt Caroline had an outfit and extra shoes in the closet, too, which she insisted would do until she arrived in Michigan.

After shopping, the girls and Aaron had lunch at Tinbell's before leaving the little town, driving the curving blacktop road through the barren winter landscape.

The day seemed gray, with no sunshine to liven the blanket of snow barely covering the stubbled cornfields and bare-branched trees.

Seated between her and Tassie in the old truck, his lap piled with packages, Rachel felt Aaron tense, gazing wide-eyed through the window at her side as they turned into his home road.

He sat quietly as the truck bumped over the frozen drive, badly rutted from the heavy fire trucks. When they stopped and the girls got out, he made no move to follow, but stared in silence, over the top of his packages, to what had been his home.

"Come on, Aaron," Tassie coaxed. "You insisted on coming—said you wanted to see it."

"I don't anymore," Aaron mumbled miserably, his gaze riveted on the black skeleton of the front silhouetted against the sky.

The front yard was littered with piles of broken window sashes and doors, tumbles of charred couch and chair frames, their upholstery gone, springs poking every which way. A pile of charred, sodden bedding sprawled at the corner of a sagging veranda frame.

"There's nothin' left. Bet even my room's gone . . . and my rock collection . . . and everything from all my life."

Aaron's voice began to tremble and he ducked his head

so his aunt and Rachel wouldn't see the tears welling up in his eyes.

"Should we go back to the inn?" Rachel inquired kindly.

"Naw, you go ahead and look," he answered. "I'll just wait here."

"I guess the reality of the fire's results hadn't registered until now," Rachel said as they approached the ruins of what had been Tassie's home.

"It was full of my entire lifetime until now," Tassie stated. "The few nice things Mama had and all the little mementoes Aaron and I had saved, all gone.

"It's strange how some little thing that had no value is missed more than the more important things."

"You mean like Aaron's rocks?" Rachel asked, noticing the strong acrid smell of burned wood.

"Yes. The house sure looks strange with the front partly burned away and the windows on the rest of it boarded up."

"Looks like this porch is intact and the kitchen area," Rachel observed as they rounded the back of the structure. "Want to go in?"

"I don't know—yes, I think I do. Mama will wonder about it."

Before she mounted the steps after Tassie, Rachel looked up at the steeply sloped roof.

"It *is* quite steep, but sure doesn't look as scary as it did during the fire," she reflected.

She noticed that a sheet of plywood covered Aaron's bedroom window. The boards around the window were charred, and oily smoke stains snaked out across the siding.

Inside the porch were piles of books and the dining set from the kitchen shoved into a corner to make room for the few pieces that had been saved from the dining room.

On the table, piled next to a broken mirror and some framed photographs, were stacks of smoke-discolored china.

"Oh, Mama's Blue Willow," Tassie said happily. "Look, Rachel, I think most of it's here. Her mama gave them to her when she and Daddy married. She'll be glad they're safe."

"We'll try to find something to put them in and take them

to her," Rachel decided, wondering what would possibly be available.

When they pushed open the warped door to go into the kitchen, the stench of ashes and old water-soaked wool carpet met them in the deep silence.

Overwhelmed, Rachel stood with her arm around Tassie's shoulder, not knowing what to say to comfort her, or what to do that would help.

"There's a flashlight in the truck," Tassie said dully. "Will you get it?"

"Sure," Rachel responded. "Be right back."

The beam of light revealed the once immaculate kitchen floor almost buried under mounds of scorched table linens and clothes. Caroline's hand-crocheted doilies were burned, and her bedroom slippers had been curled by heat and water into semicircles of leather.

Gingerly they went through the boarded-up darkness of the almost empty, water-sogged dining room to the small archway leading to the living room.

"Tassie, stop!" Rachel screamed, grabbing her friend, who was in front of her.

At their feet, just a step away, was a large gaping hole in the floor of the living room.

Quickly they drew back. Trembling at what had almost befallen her, Tassie shined the light's beam through the hole downward into the dark basement.

"Must be where it all started," Rachel speculated, shuddering. "It was fortunate Aaron had taken that little dog upstairs."

They both looked up then and saw the charred black ceiling beams.

"My room is above there," Tassie almost whispered, awe in her voice. "I'm so thankful none of us were hurt."

Picking their way back through the dining room to its door to the hallway, they stumbled over a melted radio and the ruined television cabinet that had been shoved out of the way, its glass screen completely shattered.

Carefully they picked their way to the stairway, finding it surprisingly intact, though badly scorched.

"Shall we go up?" Rachel asked.

"Might as well, I guess," Tassie replied, resignation in her voice.

The ashy water smell was stronger as they neared the top of the stairs, and once up there, they found it pitch black because of the plywood-covered windows.

Glad for the flashlight, they followed the littered hall, scattered with chunks of plaster and pieces of clothing and photographs the firemen had dropped in their haste to salvage whatever was possible, as they had downstairs.

Tassie stopped at a charred doorway and gave a small cry. Her room had disappeared, leaving in its place a smelly, wet, blackened shell.

Through an open closet door, Rachel saw a line of wire clothes hangers, nothing hanging on them now but a few shreds of cloth.

"Was this your room, Tassie?" Rachel asked, and then saw her friend nod in the dimness.

Tassie turned, leading the way back to the other end of the hall and Aaron's room.

Although it was a burned wet mess, the old heavy dresser stood against the wall, charred in spots with its mirror cracked but intact.

"May I open the drawers, Tassie?"

"Sure," Tassie said, keeping the light's beam on them. Taking a chance on finding what she wanted, Rachel bent to open the bottom drawer, trying to ignore her feeling of nausea at the stench of the fire's aftermath.

Fumbling around, she found a damp, but barely scorched, pillowcase.

Pulling it out, she gathered Aaron's plaster-dusted rocks and stones from the dresser top and slipped them into the cloth bag it formed.

Rachel opened the top drawer then and located the tightly made little wood box holding arrowheads.

"I'm ready to go," she said, putting it in the pillowcase on top of the rocks. "We better not stay any longer; Aaron might worry."

"I'm more than ready to leave," Tassie admitted. "Thanks

for coming up here with me, Rachel. At least I know for sure there's nothing left."

On Sunday, Rachel was invited with the Wolcotts to dinner at Pastor Harbrous' home after the church service. Early in the afternoon, they saw Aaron and his grandmother off on the bus that was to take them to the airport in South Bend.

"Take good care of Holly," Aaron said as Rachel hugged him goodbye. "Grandmama said I could come back and visit you and Tassie when school's out."

The early days of December were mostly clear and bright. With Tassie away at work during the day and Matthew not yet returned, Rachel had long hours alone, except for the little dog, Holly.

Following the necessary housework in the mornings after breakfast, she usually hurried through any advance preparations for the dinner she'd planned. Then she dressed warmly for a walk outside down to the river's edge, with Holly for company, to watch the still-unfrozen river moving quickly by.

Mornings after light snows, she was intrigued by the tracks she discovered of birds and small animals. Holly ran excitedly, sniffing the air.

It was on just such a morning that Rachel left the area by the hillside stairway to follow a set of rabbit tracks up over the bluff toward the back of the barn.

She still felt a little uneasy when she approached that area and generally avoided it, since the discovery there Halloween night.

But now her thoughts were on the perfectly formed little tracks in the new-fallen snow, and she barely took notice of a motor starting on the far edge of the plot around the barn.

She was engrossed, too, in thoughts of Matthew's promised return in a couple of weeks, so that she was taken completely by surprise when the trail of rabbit tracks was crossed by others.

Not rabbit tracks, Rachel decided. She stopped short, lifting her gaze, looking around uneasily. *Not Holly's either*.

The new-found tracks looked fresh, and were larger, much larger.

They appeared to be bootprints—the bootprints of a man.

Chapter Seventeen

Completely unnerved for a few moments, Rachel chided herself for being afraid just because she was near the scene of a recent murder.

Silly or not, she reasoned, *I just can't help being uneasy ... The police don't seem to have any leads as to why it happened here ... why it happened at all.*

Hesitantly, Rachel followed the large prints in their straight line toward the barn.

They seem to have come from the direction of the old lot-line fence next to the dead-end road, she observed.

Where the hijacked truck was found abandoned!

A chilled finger seemed to move up Rachel's back at the realization.

The prints are probably just from a neighbor cutting across our land ... she tried to reassure herself, as she continued following the tracks.

But if that's the case, why do they go right up to the back of the barn, then retrace back in the opposite direction?

Rachel stood perplexed, her gaze caught by the scuffled patch of snow at the spot about twenty feet away, where the large boot tracks made an about-face right at the side of the barn.

Looks like a huge broom made one sweep outward from the very edge of the barn, she speculated.

Completely bewildered, Rachel called Holly and trudged around the end of the barn and up the lane to the deserted house.

When Tassie returned from work late that afternoon, the two young women walked down the long lane and around to the back of the barn so Tassie could view the tracks and swept area Rachel had told her about.

Unable to figure it out, they returned to the house to make supper, still trying to come up with an answer.

During the following week, Rachel pushed the questions out of her mind, getting caught up in a flurry of preparations for Christmas.

Tassie had persuaded her to help with the play to be presented at the church by the youth group and with recitations by the smaller children.

The evening Tassie had a dinner date with Todd, Rachel decided to make her way up the narrow, enclosed stairs to the attic and go through items she'd not yet inventoried.

Searching through a trunk full of fabric remnants from long-ago gowns and dresses, hoping to find usable pieces from which to make doll clothes, Rachel heard again the faint movements, as though someone were up there with her.

Must be bats or mice around somewhere, she mused, avoiding the possibility of anything more threatening.

The following day she made several more trips up there, but the atmosphere differed from the evening before. Bright sunlight flooded through dusty windows, cheering Rachel as she gathered together some of the old toys she had discovered.

"We can arrange them around our Christmas tree," she told Tassie that evening while they ate. "Then maybe I'll offer them for sale in the church's booth at next summer's fair in the park."

"Too bad Aaron's not here," Tassie reflected. "I feel almost like a little kid myself, eager to look at them."

Tassie glanced through the doorway into the dining room where several boxes overflowed with dolls and teddy bears, stick toys and blocks.

"Where up there did you find them?" Tassie asked.

"In a corner behind the large wardrobe. There's a dollhouse, too, but I didn't try to carry it down," Rachel answered. "The clothes on some of the china dolls are fabulous—satins and velvets trimmed with tiny hand-crocheted lace."

Rachel chattered on, describing some of her finds, trying to cover the ache that had been growing in her heart at no word at all from Matthew.

At night she'd sleep fitfully, wondering if he wasn't coming for Christmas as he'd promised.

Why hasn't he at least let me know if his leg is improving, or whether he's decided to accept the job offer there? She plagued herself with questions, becoming more miserable with each day that passed.

Maybe he's already started working there and has decided not to make the trip back for Christmas; maybe it doesn't seem important to him now, she worried.

But surely his feelings couldn't change that fast. If I'm becoming as important to him as he said, he wouldn't feel differently in just a matter of weeks, would he? On and on her thoughts troubled her, alternating with feelings of assurance when she remembered his words to her, and frequent prayers for his good health and safety.

He means so much to me, she mused. *What would I do if he's met someone else, someone who's taken my place in his heart?*

The snowless, sunless, dreary days suited Rachel's mood perfectly.

"Looks like we won't even have a white Christmas," she grumbled to Tassie.

But nothing could dull Tassie's happiness in the love she shared with Todd, not even the absence of her family this Christmas.

She didn't know that her mother had phoned Rachel asking if her brother Jed and his wife could drive down with her and Aaron for Christmas week at the inn.

Rachel was delighted to have them, especially since her parents were both suffering from the flu and couldn't be with her, nor could she afford a plane ticket to visit them.

She said nothing to Tassie about her mother's plan, wanting to surprise her.

No reason for anyone else's fun to be spoiled just because I'm feeling down, she decided, making menus and other preparations to have a special holiday for her guests.

It was the evening before Christmas Eve day. Todd was going to bring the tree so Rachel and Tassie would have time to decorate it.

They had already hung garlands of pine boughs and tinsel on the staircase balustrade and around the big dining room.

Ribbon-tied mistletoe was hung over every doorway, and strings of colored lights outlined the veranda, lovely in the thick snow that had begun to fall an hour earlier.

Every downstairs window flaunted an aromatic wreath of green branches tucked with cinnamon sticks and star anise, and now Rachel was carefully arranging the figures of a manger scene she had found in the attic.

"It all looks so pretty, Rachel. Every room is warm and welcoming," Tassie complimented her just before the doorbell rang and she hurried to answer it.

Todd will probably appreciate something hot to drink, Rachel thought, going to the kitchen to put a flame under the pot of chocolate she had prepared.

She put a bowl of marshmallows on the table beside the chunky ironstone mugs. The sound of happy chatter and laughter drifting to her from the front of the house heightened her deep sense of loneliness.

Rachel set a plate of big raisin-oatmeal cookies on the table, then headed for the living room to greet Todd and show him where to temporarily put the tree.

But it wasn't Todd she saw leaning against the doorjamb in the open doorway. He was already lugging the large tree to a spot in the foyer corner.

It was Matthew, his hat and the shoulders of his coat white with a dusting of soft snow, his face brightening with a wide grin as his eyes met hers across the room.

"Matthew!" Rachel's voice sang out in surprised delight as she rushed toward him.

He opened his arms to greet her, both of them oblivious to the brightly wrapped packages tumbling to the floor around their feet.

His arms enfolded her, holding her close, whispering in her ear, "I've missed you so, Rachel. I've missed you so very much."

Rachel felt the heavy wool of his coat against her cheek, her tears mingling with the melting snowflakes.

Thank you, Lord, she prayed silently. *Thank you that he's safe; that he hasn't forgotten me.*

Moving away from him just enough to look up into his face, she saw her joy reflected in his eyes.

"Why didn't you tell me you were coming?" she asked, although it didn't really matter now.

"I wasn't sure I could make it at first; my leg was giving me some problems. Then, I wanted to surprise you. I swore Tassie to secrecy."

Matthew chuckled. "It looks like it worked."

"You surprised me all right," she laughed. "As for *you*, Tassie . . ." Rachel turned from Matthew's arms to see that Tassie had discreetly joined Todd in the hall.

"Tassie, will you please check the chocolate? Make sure it doesn't boil over," Rachel called, bending to gather up Matthew's scattered parcels.

"We'll join you in the kitchen," she added, placing the ribbon-tied bundles in an armchair.

When she returned to Matthew, he put his hands on her shoulders and, bending his head, kissed her gently.

"Merry Christmas, Rachel," he said softly. "Being here with you is the only gift I want—the only one I need to make me happy."

Later, after a fun visit around the kitchen table, Tassie insisted on washing the few dishes. Rachel quickly went into the living room with Todd and Matthew and told them about the expected arrival of Aunt Caroline the following evening.

It was nearly eleven o'clock by the time the fellows had the lush green tree on its stand in the bay window area.

"Be here for brunch around ten-thirty tomorrow," she called after them, as they headed for Todd's car on their way to Matthew's cottage.

"If we don't get snowed in," Matthew kidded, turning to wave when he reached the car.

"Better not," Rachel laughed. "We're having pancakes and sausages—all you can eat."

"We'll be here if I have to drag him!" Todd shouted, laughing.

The girls shut the heavy door against the cold and turned back into the cheerful room. Tassie sighed, though smiling.

"If only Mama could be here, everything would be perfect."

The following day was filled with Christmas carols from the radio and joyful fellowship. The four young people trimmed the tree and arranged packages and antique toys around it, munching throughout the early afternoon on tangerines, apples, freshly cracked nuts and the fudge Rachel and Tassie had made.

In the kitchen around midafternoon, Tassie questioned the large amount of beef chunks Rachel was browning and the big bowl of vegetables being prepared for the simple Christmas Eve supper of hearty stew they were to eat with crusty bread.

"We can always freeze leftovers for another day," Rachel said, glad she had to keep Aunt Caroline's visit a secret only a few more hours.

The aroma of browning onions and meat permeated the dining room and into the living room, drawing Matthew and Todd to the kitchen to investigate the enticing smell.

They were sniffing appreciatively near the stove when the doorbell shrilled its call.

Rachel started out of the room, then stopped.

"Tassie, will you see who's at the door?" she asked, pretending suddenly to be very busy.

A few moments later laughter and calls of greeting assured her Aunt Caroline's group had arrived. Holly and Aaron were mutually overjoyed at being together again.

Following supper, the story of Jesus' birth was read next to the little creche. Love and good cheer prevailed until late into the evening when everyone went to bed early, Matthew and Todd letting an excited Aaron accompany them to the cottage where he'd sleep in an extra sleeping bag on the floor next to Todd and Holly.

Even before they trooped into the kitchen via the back porch Christmas morning, the fellows caught the aroma of hot cinnamon rolls and brewing coffee.

The kitchen table's surface was almost hidden beneath many baking dishes and a large roasting pan holding a turkey being stuffed.

Crushed sage leaves and chopped onions added their sharp goodness to the bouquet of smells in the activity-filled room.

"Where are we supposed to eat?" Aaron piped up.

"In the dining room," Rachel directed, smiling at her little friend.

"The table's set for you and the food's on the buffet. Eggs and sausages, waffles and rolls are under covers on the warming trays," she continued.

"Oh, boy!" Aaron exclaimed, dropping his coat on a chair. "I'm starved."

"I invited Mrs. Ching to have dinner with us, Aunt Caroline," Rachel said. "But she didn't feel up to it; although she's hoping you can visit with her awhile this afternoon.

"I told her we'd bring you by with a holiday dinner. We have a basket partly packed, ready for the hot dishes."

"Thank you, honey. That's very thoughtful," Aunt Caroline remarked, giving her a hug.

"I learned it from you mostly," Rachel responded with a small laugh. "My folks were always ready to help when they heard of a need, but the idea of an individual family contributing entire dinners was something new for me."

"Well," Aunt Caroline chuckled happily, "I get as much happiness and blessing from it as our recipients do, possibly more."

"I figured that from watching you, and I experienced it for myself, too."

Following their dinner around noon and the opening of shared gifts, Aunt Caroline readied herself for her ride to Mrs. Ching's with Todd and Tassie in his big, warm station wagon.

Rachel sliced thick slabs of turkey breast and wrapped them to slip into the basket with containers of vegetables, breads and relishes.

A turkey leg was wrapped in foil, destined for another day's meal. It was tucked into another beribboned pine-cone trimmed basket next to several brightly wrapped gifts, one a large-print Bible from Aunt Caroline.

The snow had stopped and sunshine was bright on the white drifts, a lovely day for the short drive and visit.

Even before his Grandmama had departed, leaving an admonition that he not eat too much candy, Aaron was on his knees on the thick carpet investigating the antique mechanical toys and iron banks, the ancient toy cars and games.

Intrigued by them, he played happily, commenting on them to Matthew, who sat nearby.

He was propelling a metal policeman on a small vintage motorcycle around a cradle full of teddy bears when Matthew said, "Has Rachel told you that Chief Turner called one day about the mounted fish you found a few months ago?"

"No," Aaron said, still engrossed with the motorcycle. "She's probably been too busy with Christmas stuff today. What'd he say about the fish?"

"Seems the museum had already ordered a replacement by the time he contacted them about its discovery, so they said you could keep it. Saves extra paperwork for them, and you've gained a trophy for your wall."

"How about if we hang it on your wall in the cottage?" Aaron asked. "I'd like you to have it. Sort of goes with a place like that by the river. I could hang it if you'd let me."

"It's a nice looking piece of work, Aaron. Are you sure you don't want it in your own room?"

"Well, ya know, Aunt Lonnie's real nice and all, but she's sort of fussy about her house," Aaron explained. "I don't think she'd like it anyplace there."

"In that case, we'll hang it in my place, and you can come get it whenever you change your mind. A deal?"

"A deal," Aaron replied, grinning. "Okay if we do it tomorrow?"

"Sure, we'll plan on driving to the station tomorrow to pick it up."

When that time arrived, Aaron pestered Matthew to let Holly ride along.

"Not this time, pal," Matthew said. "There are several inches of snow out there; she'd drag some in on the rug before we could get her paws wiped."

"Okay," Aaron conceded, leaving a whining Holly behind as they went out the door.

The little dog was in the kitchen an hour later when they returned. At the sound of car doors slamming, she perked up her ears.

Rachel and Aunt Caroline were chatting together in the living room with Lonnie and Jed when the foyer door opened. Aaron hurriedly wiped his boots on the mat, but didn't take time to remove his coat before rushing into the living room—just in time to collide with Holly, tearing in from the back of the house.

They bumped together in front of the colorfully lighted tree, the fish flying into the air and falling on a clump of iron toys.

A small tearing, crushing sound reached Rachel's ears and she went to retrieve Aaron's prize, hoping it wasn't damaged, while he picked himself up from the floor.

"Boy, Holly, you should be on a football team," the boy laughed.

Rachel stooped to pick up the large varnished mounted fish.

The belly of the almost yard-long fish had been penetrated by the tall steeple of an iron church and the bayonet of a metal soldier.

When Rachel tried to free it, the skin covering tore even more.

"I'm sorry, Aaron. Looks like this will need some repair," she said, finally loosening and starting to lift it.

Several small plastic packets dropped to the floor as she picked the fish up.

Holding it up in both hands, Rachel tried to peer inside, then shook it.

"Well, I declare!" Aunt Caroline exclaimed, as Aaron dropped to his knees to gather up the dozens of packets that were toppling from the fish's insides.

"Let me see one of those, Aaron." Matthew was just coming into the room removing his coat.

He slumped into a chair and Aaron handed him a packet.

"Unless I miss my guess," Matthew shook his head slowly, "we're going to have a very surprised and embarrassed Chief Turner.

"Looks like he's had a hoard of cocaine sitting on his desk the past few months."

Chapter Eighteen

"Cocaine!" Rachel gasped. "Do you suppose the hijacked truck had more of it in the animal mounts?"

"Possibly," Matthew said, rising. "I'll phone Chief Turner and ask him to come out."

Although there was no need for a siren, in his excitement, Chief Turner had the one on his squad car wailing as he skimmed along the rural blacktop.

The siren getting louder as it got closer only increased Aaron's sense of the dramatic. When the car turned into the inn's drive, Holly howled along with it. Abruptly it ceased.

"I'll be . . ." Chief Turner said, after opening and checking the white powder inside one of the packets. "It's cocaine all right."

"The guys will laugh me off the force." He sounded disgruntled.

Then brightening, "One thing's for sure, though," he said to Rachel, "that murder out back of your barn is beginning to make some sense, Miss Hoekstra."

"Does this mean I gotta give the fish back again?" Aaron asked, half scowling.

" 'Fraid I'll have to keep it awhile as evidence," Chief Turner agreed.

During the rest of the week, bright with sunshine, Aaron and Holly braved the cold wind to tramp mosaics of tracks in the snow between the inn and Matthew's cottage.

"Gotta make sure she doesn't forget the note-carrying trick I taught her," he said.

"Next summer, me and Michael can have lots of fun scouting with her and Ginger."

172

"Hope he doesn't get the sniffles being out in that raw wind," his grandmother worried good-naturedly.

"Don't worry, Aunt Caroline," Rachel assured her. "My mom just always made sure I dressed warmly and gave me plenty of hot soup or chocolate when I'd come in. I always got along fine; I'm sure he will, too."

"I know," Aunt Caroline chuckled, sipping her tea. "Guess I always fussed this way over Tassie, too; it's just a mama's and grandmama's way, isn't it, Lonnie?"

New Year's Eve, Matthew and the group at the inn drove along snowy country roads into Wedgewood and the candle-lit church. There, they joined others in praising the Lord in song and welcoming in the new year with prayer.

The next day, Rachel dressed in a long red plaid skirt with matching vest to serve a farewell dinner for Aunt Caroline and Aaron, Lonnie and Jed.

"This was a farewell dinner for me, too," Matthew said to Rachel while they stood on the veranda with Tassie and Todd waving goodbye to the others.

"I was hoping you'd be staying, maybe working nearby somewhere," Rachel returned wistfully.

"Have you decided to take that job with your friend?" Todd asked as they went back indoors.

"I'm considering it more all the time," Matthew admitted. "Even though it's not what I want to do, I told Chuck I'd come for a couple of weeks, or until he can get someone to fill the vacancy there."

"Sure would have liked to find a job like the one you have, Todd. Coaching is what I feel drawn to, but I've checked with all the schools in this area."

"I'll keep my ears open," Todd promised. "If I hear of an opening, I'll let you know."

By late January, the unusually mild winter began to change with a large storm front forming on the West Coast, slowly moving east.

Up in the attic, Rachel sorted through boxes of books, arranging them in separate stacks for the Wedgewood Library, Summer Antiques Sale, and her own reading.

I suppose these won't be useful to anyone, she mused,

adding another leather-covered volume to an almost full grocery sack. *So many of their pages are ruined by moths or book lice . . . or squirrels.* Rachel smiled to herself, noticing a movement in the far corner and another store of walnuts secluded behind a box. "It's no wonder folks have thought this house was haunted if generations of you little fellows have lived in the attic and between the walls."

Putting the stack of books destined for sale in a big box labeled *Church,* Rachel added a pair of high-buttoned shoes and several lovely velvet and moire gowns she had covered with plastic garment bags.

Now, up to the turret room, she decided, glancing at her watch to make sure there was time before she had to start preparations for her and Tassie's supper.

Rachel took the key ring from her pocket as she climbed the short extra flight of stairs, then turned the larger of the two keys in the lock of the narrow door.

The room's walls, constructed of thin vertical planks of walnut, fit just so to form a circular room. There were no corners and the windows were very narrow, blending well into the smooth walls.

Reminds me of lookout slits in photos of castle walls, Rachel thought, peering down over the slant of the attic roof below.

Far below that, beyond the backyard, right next to the snow-covered mound of the root cellar, she could see the thin line of the rail fence. It snaked off to disappear among evergreen trees in the direction of the carriage house.

Rachel's gaze took in the immense sweep of landscape viewable from her vantage point.

Looking sadly neglected, the huge, once-red barn stood in the snow among clusters of tall, bare trees. Below the bluff, the river reached in both directions, moving slowly between snow-covered banks, its edges crusted with ice, glimmering in the sunlight.

Rachel turned her attention back to the little room in which she stood.

It's very quiet up here, she thought, *calm and peaceful; a fine place for a study. I wonder if it was used for that once?*

She shivered, glad she'd slipped into her heavy jacket when she'd left the attic.

Would have been too cold up here in the winter, though, with no fireplace or means of heating, she surmised, wondering at the reason for the candlesticks one in each of the seven skinny windows.

Shallow shelves, following the curve of the walls just below window height, were scattered with a collection of tattered, leather-bound books, bits of finely carved wood statuary, a few pewter dishes, and a hand telescope.

Directly opposite the door, between a pair of windows, stood a small tablelike desk. Rachel pulled the squat stool from beneath it, and, sitting down, inserted the small key from the key ring into the brass key hole on the lone drawer.

Inside were two wooden boxes, a quill pen, and a china-lidded container. The latter contained what looked to Rachel like cindery, dried ink from a long time ago.

Rachel lifted out one of the boxes and opened the lid. It contained neat stacks of currency, the bills larger in size than normal.

Perplexed, she opened the other box to find a book with a crudely hand-sewn cover and binding.

Curious, Rachel opened it and began to read the fading, spidery handwriting, disappointed that the year in the date had been smudged and was unreadable.

> May 7 River Tunnel collapsed this morning following severe flooding; will attempt to temporarily reroute. Last night a family of four; youngsters two and five. That makes a dozen souls since Easter. $20 and provisions.
>
> May 23 Two couples arrived last week. Staying so men can assist with digging.

Rachel read the notations slowly, page after page, engrossed in the unusual entries, trying to visualize what might have been happening.

> Oct. 5 Couple with tiny child all the way from Virginia. Traveling for months. Invited to stay winter, but hope to reach Canada before bitter cold weather. $15, provisions, and warm clothing.
>
> Nov. 17 Tunnel extension not holding up well; constant repairs. Badly need supply bricks and men to help.
>
> Nov. 30 Authorities plaguing us almost every week; still

suspicious. Stern warnings. Glad little or no traffic now until spring.

Dimming of the daylight coming through the narrow windows alerted Rachel to the setting of the sun.

She replaced the box of currency in the drawer and locked it. Slipping the books into her jacket pocket, she locked the turret room door behind her and hurried down to the kitchen.

I'll show this journal to Tassie after supper, Rachel decided. *It seems the owner of this house during that period wouldn't have agreed with the person who lived here later— who dressed in a Ku Klux Klan outfit.*

Darkness had fallen by the time Tassie arrived and was followed through the door by a gust of icy wind.

"It's getting colder," she informed Rachel, "and beginning to snow. I was going to make my weekly stop at Mrs. Ching's as Mama had asked, but on the way out there, a radio weather bulletin reported a heavy snowstorm building up, possibly heading our way.

"I think I'll phone her in the morning, instead, and ask if we could stock up on groceries for her before the bad weather arrives. Her usual delivery man might not be able to make it out there if snow gets too deep. Those back roads are the very last to be plowed, if at all, Mama told me.

"It was severe several years ago; the plows couldn't get through even the main highways for several days."

The next morning, Tassie awoke with a wretched headache and sore throat.

"I feel awful," she croaked, coming downstairs and dragging into the kitchen in her robe and slippers.

"Guess the germ making the rounds at work finally caught up with me."

"Oh, Tassie, I'm sorry," Rachel said, genuinely concerned. "Try to eat some of this oatmeal and I'll make some hot herb tea—is peppermint okay?"

Tassie nodded gratefully, content to be served, resting her head on her hand, elbow on the table.

"Looks like my visit to Mrs. Ching will be a couple of days late."

"May have had to be anyway," Rachel said, dishing up hot

oatmeal, adding a lump of butter and drizzle of honey to each bowl.

"I don't know how so much snow could fall in such a short time, but it looked like at least six inches a while ago, and it's still falling."

Tassie sighed. "At least I won't feel guilty now, going back to bed."

"No need to, Tassie. After all, I know the way to Mrs. Ching's, and I enjoy visiting with her. So don't worry about it."

"Thanks, Rachel." Tassie slowly stirred honey and melting butter into her cereal.

The soothing aroma of mint permeated the comfortable kitchen as Rachel brewed steaming tea, then poured a cupful for her friend.

"We could use some extra things from the supermarket, too," she said. "Especially if I may not be able to get back into town for a while."

"Matthew called—said that he hoped to be back some time this weekend, so I'm planning on having him join us for a few meals—if you don't mind."

" 'Course not." Tassie lifted her head and smiled. "I know how I feel about being with Todd whenever possible. You evidently feel much the same about Matthew."

Rachel nodded, a smile forming on her lips before she sipped her tea; then she got up to turn on the radio for the latest weather report.

Instead of the weather moderating as Rachel hoped, projections were for no let-up in the snowfall until the next day.

"I can't decide whether to drive into town or not," Rachel said. "How does the truck usually handle in the snow?"

"Fairly well," Tassie answered. "If you can get down the drive through the snow, the county crew will probably have the road plowed soon, if they haven't already. But why go out since you don't really have to?

"We can get by on simpler menus than you've planned— I'm sure Matthew won't mind. Besides, you still have things in the freezer, don't you?"

Rachel switched the radio off.

"No meat except for a large chicken, but plenty of frozen

berries and tomatoes. I think I'll go out to the root cellar and bring in more potatoes. I used the last from the pantry yesterday. I'll bring apples, too; maybe a small pumpkin for pies."

"How you going to carry all that?" Tassie's voice was raspy.

"I'll drag them in one of the gunny sacks stored out there," Rachel answered.

"Better take that shovel and the old broom you have on the back porch," Tassie suggested. "That slanted door out there is probably completely buried."

Tassie was right. Rachel tramped through the snow across the backyard to the cellar mound, and found it buried. She was glad she remembered where the door was located so she knew where to start digging and sweeping in order to uncover the door.

Inside, and down several steps, it seemed much warmer than out in the blowing, swirling snow.

Flicking on her flashlight, Rachel gathered apples and potatoes into a jute bag, enjoying the blended aromas of straw and apples.

"Hmmm, looks as though Aaron may have brought in the last pumpkin Christmas week," she surmised, pushing straw aside with her boot carefully, so she wouldn't bruise any fruit that might be there.

Moving the light beam beyond a cluster of large crocks into the far corner of the timber-supported earth room, Rachel spied another low heap of straw, gray and old looking.

She started to turn away, then leaving the sack near the door, decided to check the pile.

Moving the straw with her boot revealed nothing but a slab of wood sunk into the surface of the ground.

Disappointed, she shined the light into the crocks, finding them empty except for dust and webs.

Guess it'll be apple pie instead of pumpkin for Matthew, she decided. Grasping the top of the half-loaded sack in her gloved hands, she backed up the steps and dragged it carefully to the threshold.

A cold blast of icy wind hit her face when she pushed open the heavy door. She trudged with her head down as fast as she could through the blowing snow to the house, dragging the sack through the deepening snow.

Just as she reached the back steps, she heard the motor of a vehicle passing by on the road that went by the front of the inn.

Even if I can't get out, Matthew will be able to drive in, she realized, gratefully.

Rachel was removing her coat after leaving the sack temporarily on the porch when the phone began ringing.

Matthew! her heart sang as she raced to answer it.

But it was Mrs. Ching's wispy voice. "I'm sorry to bother you, dear, but my furnace has quit working." Rachel heard a frail cough before the elderly lady continued.

"I haven't been able to reach the serviceman; the thermometer is already down to 45 degrees. If Tassie is coming by today, I wondered if—"

"Mrs. Ching," Rachel broke in, "you'll stay here with us. Put on your coat and everything warm you can, then crawl into bed with any extra covers you have. I'll be there as soon as I can."

"Thank you," Mrs. Ching said, coughing again, her voice feeble. "Thank you."

"Make sure your door's unlocked," Rachel stressed before she replaced the receiver.

"Tassie!" she called upstairs, "I'm going to Mrs. Ching's!"

"But, Rachel, I just looked outside; the snow doesn't seem to have let up at all. I wish you wouldn't—you may get stranded somewhere."

"I have to, Tassie. Her furnace isn't working. She might get terribly sick or even freeze to death."

"Then I'm going with you!" Tassie's voice sounded even worse than Mrs. Ching's.

"No, you're not!" Rachel insisted. "I need you here. Make up a bed for her and have a heating pad and hot soup or tea ready! Thanks—Bye!"

Shrugging into an extra-heavy sweater before getting back into her down jacket, Rachel pulled on a thick knitted hat and scarf, then picked up Tassie's key from the counter.

In the foyer, she pulled a blanket from the trunk and headed out the door into the blizzard, praying silently.

Please, help me reach her in time, Lord. Make a way

through the snow for this old truck. Make me able to do whatever is needed.

The truck door creaked open, grudgingly moving on iced hinges.

Rachel climbed up into the cab, then had to get out again to clear the snow from the windshield and outside mirror.

Back inside, the cold of the plastic seat cover penetrated her jeans, making her shiver.

Rachel's frosty breath clouded her vision as she bent to insert the key in the ignition.

The old motor hesitated, then roared. "Thank you, Lord," Rachel said aloud, very slowly backing the shuddering truck through the deep snow, expecting every moment to get stuck.

But she reached the road without mishap, even through the pile of snow deposited by the plow at the drive's entrance.

Breathing a sigh of relief, Rachel headed the truck toward Wedgewood, glad the road where Mrs. Ching lived was less than half that distance.

She was glad, too, that hers seemed to be the only vehicle on the road, because so far only one lane had been cleared.

As minutes passed, she had to slow her already cautious speed as visibility became less and less.

Finally, through the swirling snow, she saw it—the small run-down barn. It was on the right side of the highway that marked the intersection with County Road 450, as well as the edge of the property on which Mrs. Ching's house sat.

Rachel slowed the truck to a crawl, preparing to make the turn. With dismay, she discovered that 450 hadn't been plowed, and snow pushed from the highway obstructed the intersection.

Now what? she wondered, tears of frustration coming to her eyes. *How will I ever reach that dear old lady?*

The thought came unbidden, because she really didn't want to go out into that freezing, swirling mass of whiteness.

Go get her. Bring her to the truck.

I'm not even sure how far away her house is; I'd never make it, she reasoned.

Then, pulling her scarf up over her mouth and nose, she wrapped the blanket over her head and around her shoulders like a poncho, and pushed the door open, slamming it shut behind her.

Rachel climbed over the pile of snow and started plunging her way through the drifts, barely able to see the fence line she was following.

It seemed like a miracle to her when she located the little house sitting far back from the road in the sea of whiteness.

Mrs. Ching was waiting for her. Rachel quickly bundled the lady's face with the extra wool scarf she had shoved into a pocket, then made sure the woman's boots were fastened securely around her heavy stocking-clad ankles.

Shutting the door behind them when they went out onto the front porch, Rachel wrapped the blanket around both of them as well as she could.

Half-supporting, half-carrying Mrs. Ching, she headed toward the road.

Several times Mrs. Ching coughed and stumbled. Rachel could hardly keep the woman on her feet in the blowing snow.

Breathing a prayer of thanks when she finally distinguished a fencepost in the whiteness and knew they had reached the road, she tried to speak encouragingly to Mrs. Chings, willing her to keep her legs moving.

"We're halfway there—it's not much farther. Keep your head down—keep going." Rachel's voice was lost in the wind.

The next time Mrs. Ching stumbled, she fell into a drift at Rachel's feet.

Rachel struggled to lift her, but Mrs. Ching was limp, unable to go one step farther. Unconscious, the little lady slipped from Rachel's grasp.

Frantically, Rachel peered into the swirling snow, the icy flakes stinging her eyes. She ducked her head, her thoughts racing as she tried unsuccessfully to lift Mrs. Ching.

The snow's like a solid wall of whiteness. I can't even see the fenceposts anymore! I wouldn't know which way to go even if I could carry her!

Rachel dropped to her knees, pulling the snow-saturated blanket over them like a flattened tent. She huddled her body around Mrs. Ching, protecting her as much as possible from the vicious cold.

Chapter Nineteen

Drowsy, her hands and feet becoming numb from the cold, Rachel thought she must be sleeping, dreaming of the fire at Aunt Caroline's house.

She listened intently to the wail of sirens mounting into a shrieking clamor as they neared.

Then silence, a deathly quiet again, with only Mrs. Ching's labored breathing to break the stillness.

Rachel remembered where she was and tried to shift her position to ease the aching in her legs.

In the distance she heard vehicle doors slamming, and after what seemed like a long while, voices, then the sound of a motor approaching very slowly.

Rachel dragged herself from under the blanket, snow creeping between her collar and scarf, and got to her knees.

"Here!" she yelled, feeling the wind was throwing the words back at her. "Over here! Help!"

Abruptly, the motor stopped; silence again.

"Help! Over here!" she called again.

"Rachel?"

Can that really be Matthew's voice? she wondered, shouting again, "Yes, we're over here!"

"Stay where you are!" another male voice called.

Half an hour later, bundled in a dry blanket in the warmth of her own kitchen, Rachel learned how she and Mrs. Ching, now receiving medical attention in Aunt Esther's front bedroom, were found.

"Matthew had driven as far as Wedgewood, and phoned to ask if we needed him to get anything on his way here,"

Tassie explained, pouring steaming mugs of coffee for those seated around the table.

"When she told me you were headed for Mrs. Ching's, I felt sure you couldn't make it back in this storm," Matthew said, continuing the story.

"Besides, she thought you should have been back by then." Matthew's eyes revealed to Rachel how worried he'd been.

Chief Turner chimed in then. "He'd made his call from the station, so when he told me about his concern, I rounded up the emergency vehicle boys and Joe, who was just coming back from his run down 84 with the plow."

"I'm sure glad you were all willing to go back out to look for us," Rachel responded gratefully. "I hope you can understand how very much I appreciate your thoughtfulness. You saved our lives."

Rachel bent her head, sipping her tea, trying to keep her tears from stealing down her cheeks.

Unsuccessful, she brushed them away, smiling. "Thank you . . . and thank you for Mrs. Ching, too."

The intense storm moved out of the area over the weekend leaving deep drifts everywhere, clogging the roads so badly that even the snowplows had difficulty getting through.

February brought more of the same, with only an occasional day of sunshine to break the monotony. Slowly, the snow began to melt.

Early days of March found the ground cleared of snow, except in deeply shaded areas, and in corners protected from sun and wind.

Crocuses and snowdrops pushed up through the cold soil, opening their cheery blooms in unexpected spots, brightening Rachel's day when she'd spot them while out walking Holly.

Rachel had spent many hours of winter's dreary, gray days going through college catalogs and studying stacks of books Tassie had picked up for her at the library. They were books about restaurant and hotel management, food handling and business techniques.

"I've about decided to take some courses down at Purdue or I.U.," she announced one evening when Matthew and Todd had been invited to join her and Tassie for supper.

"I want to make a financial success of the inn, to do the very best job with it I can. Besides having it develop into an establishment guests can really enjoy."

"That's quite a speech," Todd kidded her, "but I applaud you, Rachel."

"That goes for me, too." Matthew's eyes met hers, giving her a special message.

March slipped into history. The days for Rachel were filled with gardening, study and refurbishing of rooms.

April brought warming days, balmy evenings, lettuce, onions, radishes and tiny peas from the garden.

Easter arrived later in the month, a clear, beautiful day, the sky completely untouched by clouds. Masses of tulips and daffodils crowded the beds around the front of the inn and brightened spots around the backyard.

Rachel was feeling a bit lonely because Tassie was spending the day with Todd's family and Matthew had stayed home from church, keeping his painful leg elevated—doctor's orders.

For fun, Rachel had fixed a fancy cookie and sandwich-filled Easter basket for him, delivering it before she left in Tassie's truck for the service in Wedgewood.

"I plan to take Mrs. Ching to lunch and visit a while with her," she told him. "I'll stop by or phone later today to see how you're doing."

Rachel wished she could stay there with him, but she'd already invited Mrs. Ching, and was to pick her up on the way into Wedgewood.

"Bye, Matthew," Rachel bent to kiss him where a lock of his brown hair had fallen across his forehead.

"God bless you, Rachel," he replied softly.

Because Mrs. Ching was so reluctant to have her leave, Rachel stayed longer that afternoon than she had planned, listening to stories and looking at boxes of interesting mementos.

Accepting a photograph and tiny fountain pen as gifts when she left, Rachel shoved them into her skirt pocket.

The sky looked strange to her as she backed the truck into

the road, then a few moments later turned onto the highway.

The air seems so oppressive, Rachel thought. *Strange I didn't notice it earlier.*

The nearer to the inn she got, the darker the southern sky became.

Rachel snapped the truck radio on just in time to get the end of a weather bulletin.

" . . . watch will remain until six p.m., or until further notice." was followed by a burst of music continuing the program in progress.

Must be a storm coming, Rachel decided, pushing her foot against the accelerator.

Seems I've been out in unusual weather, of some sort or other, every season since I arrived here, she grumbled silently.

The daylight was definitely dimming by the time she parked in front of the inn and dashed inside.

Hurrying to the kitchen, she snapped the radio on and called Holly up from her place in the basement. She bounded up the stairs and into the kitchen while Rachel listened intently to the voice that had broken into a Strauss waltz.

This is a tornado warning! We recommend you take cover if at all possibe in a cellar or other protected spot. A tornado was sighted over Hooperville just two minutes ago directly over Route 84. We repeat, this is a tornado warning!

Rachel turned, heading for the still-open basement door—then she remembered Matthew.

"Matthew!" His name caught in her throat.

Will he be safe in the carriage house if the tornado comes this way? Could I help him make it to the root cellar? Rachel's thoughts raced as she hurried down the porch steps, and half-way across the yard, Holly at her heels. She paused a moment, listening. The atmosphere was deathly still. There was no movement of air, no sound of anything moving.

Without warning, everything seemed to burst into action. Leaves swirled upward from the ground, tree branches gestured wildly like giant arms.

A low rushing sound vibrated against Rachel's ears; it became difficult to breathe. Holly's whine had an eerie sound.

Rachel kicked off her pumps and began to run, sprinting toward the mound of green grass that marked the root cellar's location.

Racing to get inside when Rachel flung the door open, Holly tripped her, and they tumbled together down the few steps. The door blew shut with a heavy thud.

Surprised to find it light inside the usually dark cellar, she looked up to see a flashlight on a shelf and meet the hard gaze of a pair of pale green eyes. Rachel saw, too, the glint of a gun in the man's hand.

Momentarily forgetting the onrushing tornado, Rachel scrambled for the door.

"You're not going anywhere! Get back here! Over there in the corner!"

Holly began to whine.

"And keep that dog quiet, or put her out!"

"She's a good dog; she'll be quiet," Rachel's voice quavered as she edged her way to the corner, her hand closed over Holly's muzzle, half carrying her. Rachel wondered where she'd seen those eyes before. She remembered them from somewhere.

"What are you doing in here?" the man demanded.

"A tornado's coming," Rachel replied, noticing the man's blood-soaked sleeve. "This is the safest spot. You're hurt—can I help you?"

"Just keep your distance," he growled. "You live in that big house?"

Rachel nodded.

"Who's there with you?"

She said nothing, frightened to admit she was alone.

"I've seen others around here," he insisted. "Where are they? I said, where are they!"

Frightened now, Rachel said, "My friend's with her fiance for the day."

The man nodded, accepting her explanation.

"I'm going to turn this light off, so's I can have the battery for later. You move, I'll hear you."

"What are you going to do to me?" Rachel asked through the darkness, holding Holly close.

"Don't know . . . haven't had time to decide. Just shut up, so I can think.

"Need to get word to Margo," he mumbled to himself.

Rachel grabbed at an idea. *Get word to—a note! Holly's been taught to carry notes!*

Silently, she slipped Mrs. Ching's photograph from her pocket.

Feeling the surfaces carefully, she distinguished the slickness of the picture, and turned that side down, resting it against her knee.

Hoping the tiny fountain pen had ink in it, Rachel slipped the cap off. Visualizing the words in the dark, she positioned the pen on the photograph back and began to write.

Captive of injured gunman. Root Cellar. Rachel

Folding the stiff paper around Holly's collar, Rachel tied it in place with the narrow ribbon that held her hair back that day, carefully tucking in the ends.

"Matthew!" Rachel whispered emphatically in Holly's ear. "Go find Matthew." Holly whined, ready to play the game.

"What's going on over there? Thought I told you to keep that dog quiet!" The light flashed on.

"She wants to go out," Rachel said. "May I let her?"

"Okay, but no funny stuff," he replied.

"C'mon, Holly," Rachel stood, moved slowly toward the door, wondering if she dared try to get away.

The gun the man picked up decided for her.

"Go!" she said, shoving the door open just enough to let the dog slip out. "Go, Holly!"

"Back in the corner!" the man ordered.

Rachel returned to the pile of old straw next to the slab of wood, wondering if the tornado had passed by or whether the little dog would be injured.

Will she remember to go to the cottage? Is Matthew safe? What will happen to me? The questions tumbled over and over in Rachel's mind as the minutes ticked away. Or had it been hours? She couldn't be sure there in the pitch blackness.

Suddenly—after what seemed like forever—something pressed upward against her bare foot. Rachel reached out her hand and felt the slab of wood moving silently up, tilting as though it were a trap-door.

Her imagination took wing, soaring on wings of hope as her hands moved over it.

She coughed softly, positioning herself so her body was between the slanting slab of wood and the area of cellar where the man sat.

Sensing someone was in the space below the tilting trap-door, she attempted to let whoever was there know where the gunman was. Rachel coughed, then spoke.

"My name is Rachel . . . do you mind if I move to the other side of these crocks? I don't need your light—I can feel my way."

There was silence for a moment, then, "All right, come ahead. I don't mind you're trying to get more comfortable."

Rachel made a lot of unnecessary noise, bumping the crocks together with her foot while she extended her hand behind her back, beyond the slab of wood.

A hand touched hers, she drew in her breath.

Rachel recognized the gentle, firm clasp that released her fingers after a brief squeeze.

Her spirit was buoyed by the assurance that Matthew was near, though uncertain as to how he'd gotten there. Rachel prepared to distract the gunman in whatever way she could, so he'd think any movements he heard were hers.

"What's *your* name?" she asked loudly.

"Sal—why do you ask?"

"Just wondered," Rachel replied, keeping her voice raised, moving straw around.

"How did you get injured?"

"Argument with someone I thought was a friend," the man answered with a short, hard laugh.

"Shot me; didn't give me a chance to explain. Didn't get me in the back like he did Pete, a few months ago, though. I fooled him—pretended he'd got me in the heart. Played dead till he left, then crawled over here."

Rachel felt a hand on her shoulder for a moment, then movement in the straw between her and the man.

"Are you from around here?" Rachel asked, still keeping

her voice louder than normal, so the man wouldn't notice the extra sounds.

"Naw, out of Chicago. Pete lived around here when he was a kid. It's a secluded area, an easy route into any of the cities. Syndicate needed a spot for a new operation. Pete scouted around, found your old barn."

He nodded suddenly, "Don't know why I'm telling you this—could send me up for years."

Rachel said nothing, wondering if he was thinking of silencing her.

"May not make it out of here anyway, the way I feel," he added, as if to himself.

"What did you want the barn for?" Rachel boldly asked.

"They're using a museum setup as a front for a big cocaine operation, moving the stuff in animal hides, of all things." The man snorted, "Funny thing is, it was working till another gang trying to move in grabbed one of the trucks.

"Big guys got nervous, thinkin' the whole thing would blow apart."

The man's words were slurring. Rachel wondered if he was going to pass out—if she should try to get the gun or flashlight from him.

Where in the room was Matthew? Was anyone with him? Rachel thought of many possibilities, knowing her chance might soon pass.

A sudden flurry of movement filled the room. A light flashed on.

Rachel saw Matthew on his knees behind the man, one arm around the gangster's shoulders, trying to reach the gun in his right hand. The man's left hand held the light; he pointed both directly at Rachel.

"Down, Rachel!" Matthew shouted.

She tried to duck behind the crocks squirming face-down in the straw. She knew she wasn't concealed when she heard the gunman's, "Over there by her, now! Or she'll get the first one!"

Fear gripped Rachel and her mind went blank. She couldn't think even to pray.

Just then, the door crashed open. A man's voice yelled,

"Hold it right there!" She heard what sounded like a brief scuffle.

Rachel dared a peek over a crock.

Chief Turner and Officer Thomas were shoving a hand-cuffed man ahead of them up the steps and out the cellar door into the dusk of a calm evening.

"We'll see that shoulder gets some attention," Rachel heard Chief Turner say.

The flashlight lay where it had fallen on a potato sack, its beam illuminating Matthew trying to struggle to his feet. The knees of his slacks were gaping holes, his knee was bleeding, the bottom of the pantlegs were heavy with dirt. Rachel scrambled up to help him.

"How did you get here? What happened to your legs? And your hands! Oh, Matthew . . ." Rachel put her arms around him, under his, trying to steady him.

"Guess I'm too bushed," he admitted, slumping down onto the straw, dragging her to her knees with him.

"I came through the old runaway-slave tunnel. Your Aunt Esther's husband took me through when I was a little boy. Told me how his grandpa's family had built it before the Civil War," he explained.

"You're exhausted," Rachel said. "You shouldn't have tried it with your leg already hurting."

"I had to, Rachel," Matthew responded. "Don't you know I had to? When I read your note . . ." Matthew's voice trailed off, he pulled her into his arms, holding her close while his chest heaved as he tried to ease his breathing.

In the doorway, Chief Turner cleared his throat. "Thought this young man could probably use some help getting home." He came toward them, followed by officer Thomas, trying to avoid stepping on spilled apples.

With Matthew supported between them and Rachel leading the way, they followed the path through the rail fence gate and along the field to the carriage house.

In the early dusk, Rachel could see the field was littered with roof shingles, someone's couch and what appeared to be wood from the side of the barn.

"Storm hit hard on the outskirts of Wedgewood," Chief

Turner explained, "but it seems to have just skimmed along the top of the bluff here."

Rachel hoped the inn hadn't been damaged; Matthew's cottage seemed fine, except for some branches on the roof.

An hour or so later, after Rachel had tended to Matthew's knee and the palms of his hands and was starting to make sandwiches, she answered a knock on the door welcoming Todd and Tassie.

"What a story we have to tell you two!" Tassie exclaimed. "Or to add to what you may already know!"

"Slow down, honey," Todd chuckled.

"Well," Tassie began, "the squad car was in the drive when we arrived; Chief Turner said you were all right and explained briefly what had happened.

"And I overheard the prisoner tell the other officer that a gang had been using your barn, coming on the river using a small boat, or on the dead-end road other times."

"But I don't understand how they could come and go around there without our noticing them," Rachel reasoned.

"Ingenious idea they had," Todd explained. "That guy must have hoped he'd get leniency by telling everything, because he sure was, right in front of us, not even waiting until he'd seen a lawyer."

"What was their great idea?" Matthew asked.

"Built an invisible door into the backside of the barn," Todd explained. "Used the planks of the barn siding to make a door, weighted at the top, so it would swing outward on a pivot when a concealed bolt was removed."

"So that's what made the swept-snow spot I saw last winter," Rachel speculated.

"After the police left, Todd and I took flashlights and went out to see for ourselves, and it worked just like he said," Tassie went on. "And guess what's inside?"

"I know what's in the barn," Rachel replied.

"No, on the other side of the door you never bothered to unlock when we had the party," Tassie persisted.

"Remember, we had plenty of space and you decided to check the other area later."

Rachel nodded. "I remember now. What's on the other side? More antiques?"

"Animals!" Tassie blurted. "Mounted ones, and animal skins and wire armatures of all types and boxes of clay and plaster, too."

"Appeared to be a taxidermy business," Todd continued. Turning to Matthew, he added, "If they were using them in the same way they did the fish you told me about, they must have had the potential of millions of dollars."

Matthew shook his head, thinking of at least one life lost because of greed for those dollars. "I'll live on a coach's salary any day," he said. "Have you made a decision yet, Todd?"

"Yes, just yesterday. Tassie and I plan to move to a little town near Elkhart where I'll coach, and Joe Barnes will leave the Wedgewood school system for my spot at Hooperville.

"We've both put in a good word for you with the Wedgewood Board; they'll be contacting you this week."

"Glad that's about settled," Matthew confessed. "It's been my first choice as my life's work.

"I guess the next thing on the agenda," he added casually, "is to marry Rachel so I can take care of her and hopefully keep her from the dangerous situations she's always getting into."

Tassie and Todd laughed lightly and Matthew grinned at Rachel, raising his eyebrows questioningly. But Matthew's eyes weren't laughing, though they sparkled with a special joy.

When she met his gaze, Rachel saw his love for her, the love she knew he was going to tell her about tonight.

Her heart beat faster as she realized she would very soon hear his voice say, "I love you, Rachel; marry me." *After supper, after Todd and Tassie have left and I'm ready to walk to the inn with Holly, that's when he'll tell me,* she supposed, pulling her gaze away from his gray eyes.

A radiant Rachel, flushed with excitement, stepped into the small kitchenette to make extra sandwiches.

Or, maybe I'll tell him first. A small smile touched the corners of her lips as she spread butter on dark bread.

Yes, that's it! I'll say, "I love you, Matthew . . . I want to be your wife."